S0-AYO-341

JAN 0 7 2008

SUNSET TRAIL

This Large Print Book carries the
Seal of Approval of N.A.V.H.

SUNSET TRAIL

A WESTERN DUO

WAYNE D. OVERHOLSER

THORNDIKE PRESS

An imprint of Thomson Gale, a part of The Thomson Corporation

THOMSON

GALE™

Detroit • New York • San Francisco • New Haven, Conn. • Waterville, Maine • London

LIBRARY OF CONGRESS CATALOGING-IN-PUBLICATION DATA

Overholser, Wayne D., 1906–1996.
  [Twelve hours till noon]
  Sunset trail : a western duo / by Wayne D. Overholser.
    p. cm. — (Thorndike Press large print western)
  ISBN-13: 978-0-7862-9968-3 (alk. paper)
  ISBN-10: 0-7862-9968-1 (alk. paper)
    1. Large type books. I. Overholser, Wayne D., 1906–1996. Sunset trail.
  II. Title.
  PS3529.V33T84 2007b
  813'.54—dc22   2007030485

Published in 2007 by arrangement with Golden West Literary Agency.

Printed in the United States of America on permanent paper
10 9 8 7 6 5 4 3 2 1

SUNSET TRAIL

SUNSET TRAIL

I

It was May 1846, and Independence, with civilization behind it and wilderness ahead, teemed with savage life. A common trail stemmed westward and split. One branch bore up the Platte and across South Pass and on to Oregon; the other stretched toward the Arkansas and forked at Cimarron Crossing, one road following the river to Fort Bent where it angled south, the other taking the dry route across the terrible *Jornada del Muerto,* the Journey of the Dead Man

Along these trails the decision for empire would be made. In the northwest the British still held their claim to the Oregon country. At Santa Fé swashbuckling *Don* Manuel Armijo strutted in his gold braid and crimson sash and ruled with the same cruel hand that had marked so many Mexican governors of the past.

Bruce Shane, standing on the corner of

Courthouse Square, listened absent-mindedly to the wagoners' thundering oaths. He thought sourly that, except for the foreign agents who worked beneath the surface here in Independence, there were few indeed who realized that the destiny of a great nation would be decided out there in the plains and mountains, along the roads that were little more than wheel ruts of loaded Conestogas.

A tall lithe man was Bruce Shane, as capable of playing the fast game as the slow one, as much at home visiting in a Ute lodge as in the White House in Washington. He had returned only the day before from Washington, his mind heavy with the importance of the mission that had been given him. Discarding the clothes of polite society, he had donned his worn buckskins, slid his Green River knife and Colt revolving pistol into his belt, and turned back a page in his book of life.

"How thar, Shane!" a man called. "Heerd you was in Washington. Confabin' with the big bucks."

Bruce wheeled to the mountain man who had come up behind him. "Bill Purdy!" he bellowed. "What are you doing in civilization? Get lost?"

"Reckon so." Purdy motioned to the

turmoil in the street. "Ain't heerd so much cussin' since I was hyar the last time. That what you call civileezashun?"

"Sure. You've got to be mighty civilized to cuss like a muleskinner."

Purdy sniffed. "I'll take a cañon where you don't heer nuthin' but a Ute war whup. This kentry's goin' to the devil. Wasn't no crowd like this the last time I was hyar."

Purdy stared disdainfully at the street. He was a small wiry man, his face as wrinkled as an overripe apple, filled with a restlessness that had driven him from the Río Grande to the Columbia. The ashes of his thousands of campfires made an aimless trail through mountains and prairies. Hungry for white man's "fixin's" he had come to Independence only to find he had no stomach for it.

"Won't be long till those cañons will be gone," Bruce said soberly. "The country's on wheels this year."

"Danged if hit ain't. The creeks're trapped out, and beaver's down to a dollar a plew."

"I've got a job for you, Bill."

"You know me better'n that, Bruce." Purdy turned a hurt face to him. "I kin still tell fat cow from pore bull. Long as I kin, I ain't takin' no job in this hyar mess you call civileezashun."

"Let's have a drink."

"Thet shines." Purdy's bearded face softened under a grin. "Muley Mogan's got some skull varnish thet'll take the hide right offen your gullet."

They pushed through the milling crowd, Bruce mentally cursing himself for his mistake. He should have known that his abrupt mention of a job would have slashed the oldster's pride, but his mind had been on other matters. He needed Purdy, and, now that he took time to think about it, he knew there was only one way to get the mountain man's help.

Bruce, who had known Independence for years, had never seen it like it was this spring of 1846. Emigrants for Oregon waiting for the grass. Traders. Mountain men in fringed buckskins. Dragoons from Fort Leavenworth. Gamblers. Adventurers staked by relatives who lacked the courage to risk the wilderness, *voyageurs* from the north country. Thieves and killers wanted by the police of a dozen nations. Sky pilots who preached of a fiery hell. Hard-faced women looking for anything that would better their lives. Blanketed Indians of the friendly tribes.

This was Independence, doorway to empire. A finger pointing westward. Cradle of men's dreams. Hodge-podge of humanity. Here was the essence of life: marriage for those who had cast their lot together and refused to wait, birth on the trail with a dusty blanket for a bed and the sky for a roof, perhaps death and a sagebrush grave. This was where the timid had their first and only look at the frontier, where the daring cut the shackles society had forged and rolled out into the unknown to mold their own destiny. Gamblers preyed on the unwary, stripping them of the money that might make a dream come true. Violence, then, and blood and flashing Green River knives. The smell of powder and the stink from the mule markets.

Out there was the untamed wind and land that reached to the sky. Thirst and starvation and the scalping knife. And farther, if there was still life, was the treasure, out there toward the sunset. Oregon by one road. Santa Fé by the other.

That was the run of Bruce Shane's thoughts as he stood with Bill Purdy at the bar in Mogan's Saloon. He had his place in this, a vital place given him by officials in Washington, but two men had twice as much chance of carrying out the perilous mission assigned him as one.

"You know a man named Ed Catherwood?" Bruce asked.

"Yup." Purdy gnawed off a chew of tobacco and tongued it into his cheek. "Seen him jest tuther day. Headin' fer Santy Fee soon as the grass is up. Him and his pard, Curt Glover. Got a big outfit."

"They have a store in Santa Fé, don't they?"

"Yup," Purdy repeated. "Catherwood's a square 'coon. Ain't shore 'bout Glover."

"Where'll I find Catherwood?"

"Got a cabin at the edge o' town. Him and his kid Mick." Purdy rolled his quid to the other side of his mouth. "What're you drivin' at?"

"I've been looking for Catherwood," Bruce said evasively. "Who's guiding their train?"

"Catherwood don't need no guide. Been over the trail so much he could go it blind." Purdy turned and spat. "Glover asked me to go with 'em, but don't reckon I hanker to see Santy Fee this year. Might go fur as the Cimarron Crossin'."

"Reckon they'd take me?" Bruce asked casually. "Had a notion lately I wanted to see Santa Fé."

"I'll give Catherwood a push," Purdy promised. "He kin use another rifle." He lowered his voice. "Y'er crazy to go to Santy

Fee this year. Eff thet's the way a man's stick floats, then it's what he's got to do, but you'll shore lose your ha'r."

"It fits pretty tight."

"Not tight enough with buffler plumb scerce like they is. Every tribe on the plains is honin' fer trouble." He brought his mouth close to Bruce's ear. "We're fixin' to fight Mexico shore as my rifle shoots center. A Yankee in Santy Fee ain't gonna stay healthy long."

"What's the talk in Santa Fé and Taos about Armijo?"

"*Wagh!* All shiny brass and no guts." Purdy turned to spit again. "Some gab 'bout separatin' and formin' a Republic o' their own."

Bruce would have told him then if Armadillo Dunn hadn't come in. A swell-chested bull of a man, Dunn could break an enemy's spine with two hands and a knee, and do it with as little feeling as he'd wring a pigeon's neck. He paused inside the door, muddy brown eyes sweeping the room. Seeing Purdy, he came toward him in a rolling walk, meaty lips holding a malicious grin.

"How thar, Purdy," Dunn rumbled.

Purdy swung away from the bar, hand darting to his knife, but he was too slow. Moving with surprising speed for so big a man, Dunn clutched Purdy's right wrist as his other hand jerked the oldster's coonskin cap from his head.

"Wa-al, I'll be damned," Dunn crowed. "No ha'r, Purdy."

Bill Purdy had lost his hair years ago to the Comanches and they had left him for dead at Point of Rocks. It was a matter of intense shame with him, and he always wore his coonskin cap regardless of the occasion. His friends understood and ignored it, but Armadillo Dunn was no friend. Bruce had never heard how the trouble between them had started, but it went back over the years.

Purdy cursed, tried to pull free, and failed. He reached for his knife with his left hand, but Dunn jerked him forward and brought a great fist swinging upward in a blow that held the power of a mule kick. The old man's teeth *clicked* together and he went down as if he'd been clubbed with a gun barrel. He fell flat, the sun from a front window shining on his horribly scarred head.

"Ain't much left o' thet old coot." Dunn's muddy eyes fixed on Bruce. "Might as well go find a hole and die."

Armadillo Dunn had held a bad name along the frontier for years. On at least two occasions he had hired out as guide, his caravan had been attacked by Indians and destroyed, and he'd been the only one to get back to Independence. He'd claimed that he'd had a fast horse, and, when he'd seen that it was all up with the wagon train, he'd broken through the ring of savages and escaped, an explanation which was less than convincing.

Nobody had fought Armadillo Dunn and won. Most had died or been maimed for life. Bruce knew that, and he knew he had a bigger job than brawling in a saloon, but he wasn't a man to stop and reason at such a time.

Bruce hit Dunn in the face, a looping blow that staggered the big man. He hit him again, driving him back across the room and upsetting a card table. Men scattered before him, and formed a circle. Someone yelled: "Give him Green River, Shane!"

No one liked Dunn. He was a coyote in a grizzly's body, a killer and probably a thief and traitor, but there was none to see that Bruce Shane got a fair fight. It was the two of them now. No rules. A primitive struggle, perhaps with death for the loser, or at best the loss of his eyes.

Now Dunn held his ground, using his weight to force Bruce back, taking a dozen blows so that he could give one. He could afford to fight that way, knowing his greater strength and weight would eventually wear his lighter enemy down.

Bruce sledged the squat man on the nose, felt the squish of flesh and saw the spurt of crimson. He cracked him on the side of the head, blacked an eye, and smashed him on the jaw. Still Dunn's grin clung to his wide battered mouth, a grin that said he'd never been knocked out and Bruce Shane wasn't the man who could do it. He kept crowding, needing but one chance. One good chance, and he'd take this punishment to get it.

It came when Bruce slipped, his swinging right making a complete miss. Dunn got him then, a ham-like fist cracking against the side of his face. A million lights flashed across Bruce's brain. He fell, but he didn't go out.

A man yelled: "He'll get your eyes, Shane!"

Prodded by the words, Bruce rolled, heard Dunn drop on his knees, and curse. He'd aimed to smash Bruce's ribs.

Coming to his feet, Bruce rubbed a hand across his blurred eyes, and backed around a card table.

"Stand up and fight!" Dunn roared, lunging around the table in pursuit.

Still Bruce retreated, keeping away from those outstretched hands that would snap his neck once they had fastened upon it. Slowly his head cleared and, reversing his tactics, came at Dunn, moving swiftly and unexpectedly. Lowering himself and turning, he pulled the man's arm over his shoulder and twisted. Dunn flew over Bruce and crashed onto the floor, wind gushing out of him in a yeasty sigh.

There was that one short moment when Dunn lay paralyzed, lungs laboring for breath, long enough for Bruce to drop upon him exactly as Dunn had aimed to do a moment before. Again wind spurted out of the man. Ribs caved under Bruce's knees. A downsweeping fist cracked Dunn's jaw.

"Give him Green River, you fool!" Purdy shrilled. "He'd slit your gullet eff he had a chance."

The knife was in Bruce's hands, the point against Dunn's throat. Terror was in the man's bulging eyes, in the whimper that broke out of him.

"I wouldn't do that," a man said, a soft voice Bruce had never heard before.

"Let him have it!" Purdy cried.

Bruce came to his feet. It wasn't in him to knife a man who lay helplessly under him.

"Get out of town, Dunn," Bruce grated.

"Next time I'll kill you."

Dunn lumbered to his feet. Still laboring for breath, he moved in his rolling gait to the door.

"You fool," Purdy growled. "He'll git you in the back shore."

Bruce paid no attention. He was looking at the soft-voiced man who had spoken to him. His eyes and hair were black, his face inscrutable. No buckskins for this man or ordinary linsey. He wore black broadcloth and a fine beaver hat, a handsome polished man with none of the frontier roughness about him.

"So you sided Armadillo Dunn," Bruce said evenly. "I reckon you're the only man in Independence who would."

"You won your fight," the other said. "There's no sport in cutting an enemy's throat when he's helpless. I'd have said the same if you'd been underneath."

"What's your interest in Dunn?"

"I have no interest in him."

"I wouldn't have slit his gullet," Bruce said hotly, "though he had it coming, but I don't like another man telling me how to fight." He laid a hand on his Colt butt. "Maybe you'd like to back your talk with lead."

"I never brawl unless there is a reason.

When there is, I kill a man. I have no reason to kill you." The man nodded, his veneer of courtesy a mask to cover his feelings, and shouldered his way through the ring.

"You dang' idjit!" Purdy cried witheringly. "You let Dunn walk out."

But Bruce wasn't listening. He was watching the black-eyed man walk in an unhurried pace to the door. When he was gone, Bruce asked: "Who is he?"

"Calls himself Wade Flint," a bullwhacker said. "Been lookin' for a way to get to Santy Fee. I hear Curt Glover's takin' him."

"Let's have another drink of Mogan's skull varnish." Bruce turned to the bar, wondering if Ed Catherwood knew about Wade Flint.

Retrieving his coonskin cap, Purdy pulled it over his ears. "The arrer ain't feathered yet thet'll fix this 'coon," he bragged. Then his pale agate eyes narrowed. "Shane, if thet varmint figgered to git me, he wouldn't have tackled me like he done."

"I was thinking that," Bruce agreed.

"He knowed you'd pitch in, and you was the one he was arter." The old man pulled at his beard, keen mind giving thought to this idea. "When thet critter passes this 'coon up to git you, it ain't sense."

"Makes sense if he aimed to fix it so I'd

start the ruckus. It adds up to something, Bill."

"Somebody's puttin' out good beaver to git you planted afore the wagons pull out," Purdy guessed, "and don't want nobody to know you're the 'coon they're arter."

"That's my hunch." Bruce downed his drink. "Let's go find Catherwood."

II

Covered wagons had been rumbling into Independence for more than a month, had fanned out along the bluffs above the Missouri, and now their white Osnaburg tops glittered in the evening sunlight, the smoke of their cooking fires moving with the breeze. The show still went on in the street; lunging kicking mules adding their squeals to the din, wheels and hoofs making a sucking sound as they were pulled free from the deep ooze of the street, wagon *creaks* and harness *jangle,* the *crack* of the bullwhips and constant volleys of oaths, and now and then the roar of a gun piercing the racket.

It was an old scene to Bruce Shane and Bill Purdy. They bucked the crowd, barely conscious of the storm around them, the fight with Armadillo Dunn and the reason for it still crowding their minds.

"You could find Catherwood easy," Purdy said suddenly as they came out of the crowd. "Any coot in the town could tell you."

"I didn't ask anybody else because I didn't want folks knowing I was looking for him. I told you I had a job for you. Uncle Sam needs your help."

"*Wagh!* Then I'm your 'coon."

"Catherwood and Glover have ordered a big shipment of guns, something they've never done before. The War Department wants it investigated. If those guns get to the Comanches, there'll be hell to pay. Or to the Pueblo Indians and greasers around Santa Fé."

"Thet don't shine." Purdy shook his grizzled head. "What're we gonna do?"

"Keep those guns from going through. It won't be easy because we aren't fighting Mexico yet, but if they get to Santa Fé before the war breaks out, Kearny will have a hell of a lot of trouble. A hundred guns could hold Apache Cañon."

"Thet don't sound like Ed Catherwood."

"That's why I want to see him, but I don't want the whole town knowing it. I'm after the boss man, and I don't want to scare him off."

Presently Purdy said: "Thar's the cabin."

"Smoke's coming out of the chimney. Somebody's there."

"The kid Mick mebbe, but Ed'll be along eff he ain't thar now." They came up the muddy path, and Purdy called: "How thar, Ed!"

When there was no answer, Purdy shouldered the door open, and stopped abruptly. Bruce, looking over his shoulder, felt his muscles tighten. Ed Catherwood sat hunched forward at the table, head down, a knife driven hilt deep into his back.

"Stay where you are."

It was the Catherwood kid. Clad in buckskins, the boy stood at the table, his face as gray as the wing of a goose. He couldn't have been more than sixteen.

"No sense in thet talk, Mick," Purdy snapped. He came on to the table. "When did you find him?"

"A little while ago," the boy said tonelessly. His blue eyes fixed on Bruce with a strange hate-filled stare. "He's been dead two, three hours."

"Any clues?" Bruce asked as he moved out of the doorway to stand with his back to the wall.

"Maybe!" the boy cried. His hand came up in a swift rhythmical motion. A knife made an arc through the air, the blade shining brightly as it whipped through a golden slash of sunshine. There was the *thud* of steel in wood, and Bruce Shane was pinned to the wall.

Purdy made an open-palm swipe at the kid and missed because the boy stepped back, pistol palmed. "You daft?" Purdy raged.

"Not daft, Bill." The kid threw a wad of paper on the table. "I found that in Dad's hand."

"You hurt, Shane?" Purdy asked, picking up the paper.

"He got mostly sleeve." Bruce jerked the knife from the wall. "Let's see it, Bill?"

Purdy flattened out the paper and passed it to Bruce. Printed in ink were the words: **Bruce Shane.** He lifted his eyes to the boy's. "I didn't kill your father, kid. If you'd use your head, you'd know I wouldn't leave this."

"Dad wrote it." The boy motioned to the quill pen and bottle of ink on the table. "After you made wolf meat out of him."

"He wouldn't write anything," Bruce said sharply, "with a knife in his back like that."

"Wouldn't take long to write two words," the boy said stonily.

"Did your dad usually print or write out what he had to say?"

Mick Catherwood's eyes flicked to Purdy and back to Bruce. He took his time to answer as if this was a thought that had never occurred to him. He was thin, almost skinny, with a tanned face that held a scattering of freckles and a dimple in a defiant chin. He was younger than Bruce had first thought, probably not more than fourteen, with features that were almost feminine.

"He never printed," Mick said at last.

"Then why would he print this?"

"I don't know." Mick pointed to the knife. "Yours?"

"Never saw it before." Bruce stepped to the dead man and stared at the knife. The initials **BS** were carved on the handle. He brought his gaze to the boy's face. "Kid, I can't tell you my reasons, but I'm the last man in Independence to want your father dead. I came here to talk to him."

"You're lying," Mick snarled.

"Shane ain't no coot to lie," Purdy said sharply. "I been with him 'most all afternoon. He didn't do it."

Again the boy's gaze came to the old mountain man's face. He struggled with suspicion for a moment, but he knew Bill Purdy too well to doubt his word.

"All right." Mick lowered his pistol. "If Shane didn't do it, who did?"

"I shore cain't guess," Purdy said somberly. "Kin you, Shane?"

"It was likely someone who knew your father," Bruce said. "If I'm reading the sign right, they were sitting here at the table talking something over."

"Mebbe them guns . . . ," Purdy began.

"Probably about the wagon train," Bruce cut in. "Then the killer got up and walked around." He pointed to the cigar ashes on the floor. "Your dad smoke cigars?"

"He smoked a pipe."

"The killer got behind him and gave him the blade when your dad was looking the other way, not thinking of anything like this. If you believe I did it, you can make so much trouble that I'll have to get out of town."

"Eff you don't git your neck stretched first," Purdy added.

"If you keep still about it, Mick," Bruce went on, "I'll have the killer and the reason for him murdering your dad. That's a promise."

Mick ran a buckskin sleeve across his eyes. "Dad didn't have any enemies. Didn't even cheat the Indians. Nobody had any reason to do this."

"These are hard times," Bruce said. "More things are going on than most of us realize.

The reason might not have been anything personal."

"You know what it is?"

"I think so. If you give me your word to keep still about this fake evidence against me, I'll give you my word to get his killer."

"His word's good," Purdy said.

Again it was faith in the old mountain man that settled the question. Mick nodded. "All right, Shane."

"You better come with us," Bruce said.

"I'm staying here," Mick said flatly. "You find Glover, will you, Bill?"

"I'll nab him fust thing," Purdy promised.

When they were on the muddy trail back to town, Bruce said: "Don't spill that about the guns to anybody, Bill. I figured you knew enough to keep your mouth shut."

Purdy cursed. "It jest slipped out. Ain't got a brain in my haid." He gnawed off a chew of tobacco and tongued it into the side of his mouth. "What notion hev you got 'bout Ed?"

"I'd seen Catherwood, though I didn't know him well. I never have seen Glover, but I'm remembering you said you weren't sure how square he was."

"I dunno nuthin' 'gainst him," Purdy said uneasily. "He ain't been with Catherwood long. Came from New Yawk, I heerd."

"But he's a man who wouldn't hesitate at making a big stake, even if it meant freighting guns and powder to the Comanches. Or to the bunch that's talking about a republic in Santa Fé. Or Armijo if there was enough in it."

Purdy spat into a mud hole. "My brain is shore dried up. You're sayin' Ed wouldn't stand fer their train haulin' the guns and callin' 'em grub 'n' sech."

"Would he?"

"No, Ed wouldn't. Thet don't shine."

"When you find Glover, tell him I want to ride with him."

"I'll tell him. And eff you git to Santy Fee, they'll cut off your ears and nail 'em to the wall like they've done better coots'n you."

III

Bruce had supper that night with Aunt Sukey Milder who ran the Good Grub Restaurant. He went back into the street and moved with the crowd for a time, speaking to men he knew. Most of them were trappers planning to return to the mountains. But some had hired out to guide wagon trains across the plains.

"Polk's fixin' to give us a war," one said. " 'Bout time, too. I wouldn't mind shootin' a few Britishers arter the way they cleaned beaver off the cricks."

"The good days air behind us," another said somberly. "You don't see no buffler this side of the Little Arkansas. The greenhorns air comin' in white tops faster'n you kin count, carryin' plows to dig hell out of the dirt."

He was standing, Bruce Shane thought, in the shadow of a disappearing past. They were a breed to themselves, these mountain men, clad in fringed buckskins stained by grease and sweat and blood till it shone like polished leather. Armed with Green River knives and Hawkins rifles. Sharp with the savvy that it took to survive on lake or river or in an untamed land. They were the mountain men watching their life being cut out from under them, but still they were Americans. If needed, they'd say, as Bill Purdy had said: "*Wagh!* Then I'm your 'coon."

Bruce drifted along the street, in and out of saloons, watching for Purdy and wondering if he had found Curt Glover. He looked, too, for Armadillo Dunn and Wade Flint, but he saw neither. He turned back to Aunt Sukey's and the room she kept for him.

Perhaps he was not as cautious as was his habit, for his mind was seldom away from what he had learned in Washington and the task that had been assigned him. But no amount of caution could have stopped the ambusher's bullet. It came from the darkness just before Bruce reached Aunt Sukey's door, the *crack* of the rifle from across the street slapping into the town racket, the flash ribboning the night and fading.

The bullet swiped at Bruce's side, gouging out a strip of lean meat along a rib. He dropped into the mud, drawing his gun as he went down. He fired three times, targeting the spot where the rifle had flamed. The man must have had a double-barreled piece, for he shot again, a wild bullet this time that ripped into the corner of Aunt Sukey's house.

There was silence then except for the sounds of brawling that flowed along the street from the saloons. Bruce thought he had hit the man, but he had no way of knowing whether he had killed him. He waited, his side aching dully, blood a warm pool along his ribs.

The nature of the town this time of year was such that the shooting attracted no attention. It was merely another noise dropped into a pool of racket. Presently a bullwhacker came along the street, reeling under the numbing influence of the milky

31

liquid sold for whiskey. He stumbled over something and fell into the mud. Slowly he regained his feet, cursing because dead men were all over town, and stumbled on.

Bruce crossed the street, gun still palmed, and found the ambusher. The man was dead. Bruce drew him into a finger of light that slanted across the mud from Aunt Sukey's window and discovered that he was a renegade known along the frontier as Snake River Joe.

Retracing his steps, Bruce saw with striking clarity that somebody wanted him dead, but he didn't know why. Only Bill Purdy knew the reason for his being in Independence, and Purdy wouldn't talk. Not after the slip he'd made to Mick Catherwood. There could be, then, only one other answer. There had been a leak in Washington, and word of his mission had been passed halfway across the continent.

Aunt Sukey clucked and took on over his wound, washing and bandaging it, and ordered him to bed.

"I can't make you out," she said worriedly. "Got all the book larnin' a man can have. Cavortin' with politicians and sech, but here you air, takin' off your fancy duds and wearin' buckskins, and fixin' to git your ha'r lifted."

"Just crazy," Bruce admitted.

He went into his room and came to a flat-footed stop. Somebody had broken a window and had gone through his things. Clothes were dumped into the middle of the floor. Linings had been ripped out. Bureau drawers had been flung into the corner. Even a pair of moccasins had been slashed to pieces. But Bruce grinned as he took off his hat and laid it on the bed. As long as he was conscious, he'd have his hat, and his enemies would not find what they sought.

Despite the throbbing burn in his side, Bruce slept well. He was having breakfast when Bill Purdy brought in a big man who was a stranger to Bruce.

"Shane, this hyar is Curt Glover." Purdy motioned to the trader. "I sez Bruce Shane wants to ride to Santy Fee, and he figgers he'll git his ha'r lifted eff he rides down the trail alone. Glover sez shore. We'll give him a job to boot."

Bruce shook Glover's hand. The trader was a massive heavy-boned man with hazel eyes and a genial manner that seemed genuine.

"I've heard of you, Shane." Glover sat down across the table. "Go ahead with your eating. I won't take more'n a minute. I don't mind saying I was happy to learn you wanted to go to Santa Fé. I've been over the trail, but always by Bent's Fort. This time we'll take the Cimarron Crossing." He took off his beaver hat and rubbed his round baldhead. "I don't like it. That damned *Jornada del Muerto* scares me to hell 'n' back, but it saves me some miles, and I'm anxious to get back to Santa Fé."

"I've never been over the *Jornada*," Bruce said with regret. "I'd like to take the job, but I wouldn't be much good."

Glover showed his disappointment. "I'd counted on you, Shane. Heard a lot about you."

"Like what?"

"That you're a good hand with Injuns and that's what counts. We'll have fifty men with about twenty-five wagons. It ain't so many if two or three hundred Pawnees go after our stock."

"Or eff the Comanches take a likin' to your ha'r," Purdy added.

"Catherwood always handled that end of things," Glover said. "He'd been in business in Santa Fé for years and always freighted his own stuff across. What happened to him is hell and nothing less. He was the backbone of the business. I'm not one to

34

deny that."

"What about the kid?" Bruce asked.

"Mick'll go along." Glover's eyes fixed on Bruce as if he was wondering about something. Then, lowering his gaze, he reached for a cigar. "Mick has half the business, of course. And he's damned sharp for a kid. He'll hold up his end of things."

"I'd like to go with you," Bruce said. "Another rifle will come in handy."

"I'll want you to run the outfit. We'll pay one hundred dollars a month." His face clouded. "But how in hell will we get across the *Jornada?*"

"Bill knows the dry route like he does the path to his mouth. Why not take him along?"

"Sure," Glover agreed without hesitation. "I'll pay him the same."

"I don't want the job," the mountain man blazed. "Thar's some thet cain't tell fat cow from pore bull. They kin take the guidin' jobs, but. . . ."

"This is different," Bruce cut in. "We'd never make it across the *Jornada* without you."

Suddenly Purdy remembered. Or he might have stated his objection as a matter of principle. He shrugged as if giving in. "All right, Glover. I was jest thinkin' thet eff the

35

Injuns do lift our ha'r, they'll have a hell of a time with you 'n' me."

Glover laughed. "That's right." He stepped to the fireplace, and lighted his cigar. "Pay starts today, Shane. We'll roll out in the morning."

"The grass ain't up," Purdy objected.

"Up enough. We'll take some feed along." Glover scowled, the veneer of amiability momentarily rubbed from him. Then, as if remembering his rôle, he straightened and smiled, pulling hard on his cigar. "We're using mules, Shane. Can't afford to waste time waiting on the grass. We'll hold over at Council Grove and see that everything is in good shape before we jump off."

"It ain't gonna be no pleasure jaunt," Purdy warned. "I heerd Kearny has pulled out with three thousand Dragoons. He ain't goin' arter buffler."

Glover wheeled on the mountain man, eyes green with sudden fury. "He doesn't have that many men. You're lying, Purdy."

"Lyin'?" the old man squalled. "Great hell amighty, Glover. You ain't big enough to make me lie. I'm jest tellin' what I heerd."

Glover paced around the table and came back to the fireplace, cigar ash breaking loose and falling to the floor. When he faced Bruce, he had regained his composure.

"If it's true, it may be bad for us. Armijo will drive every Yankee out of Santa Fé or throw us into the *calabozo*." Glover pounded a fist on the table until the dishes rattled. "They talk about destiny. About fighting England for Oregon. Hell, all we've got is a raggle-taggle army and a two-bit fleet. If Polk didn't want to make a name for himself, we could tend to things out here ourselves."

"Like setting up a republic in New Mexico?" Bruce asked.

Glover's eyes narrowed. "Why do you ask that?"

"It's what Texas did. There's talk of the same thing happening in California."

"Perhaps it's the answer," Glover said carefully as if it were a new thought. "Armijo is a poor thing for a governor. We're tired of being overtaxed and misruled and kicked around by him. It was a sore point with Catherwood, and I've wondered if it had anything to do with his murder."

"Why do you think it might?" Bruce asked with sudden interest.

Again Glover paced around the table. "I'll expect you to respect my confidence, Shane. Ed Catherwood was engaged in a separatist movement. I'm opposed to it myself because, if it fails, it'll be the end of Yankee trading in Santa Fé. Catherwood made no secret of his feelings, and he was a dangerous man to Armijo." Glover paused, and added bitterly: "Armijo has a long arm with plenty of money he's stolen from us traders to hire a hundred killings."

"It's possible," Bruce murmured.

"I've got to dust along." Glover reached for his hat. "We're burying Ed this afternoon. The job of running the outfit is yours. I understand you and Purdy are friends so I don't expect any disagreements between you after we cross the Arkansas."

"I'll take Bill's word on the *Jornada*," Bruce said.

Purdy waited until the door closed behind Glover. Then he came to the table, his grizzled face showing a pressing anger.

"Call me a liar, will he?" Purdy shook his fist at the door. "Shane, you want to know who's runnin' the outfit. I'll tell you. It's thet varmint who tried to pull you off o' Dunn in Mogan's Saloon."

"Flint?"

"That's him. Arter we pulled out o' Catherwood's cabin, I started huntin' fer Glover. I seen him in Finneran's saloon lappin' up some blue ruin with Flint. He wasn't real surprised when I told him 'bout Catherwood. Then I sez you wanted to go.

He looks at Flint 'n' Flint nods. That's when Glover sez you kin guide. I tell you he's crookeder'n a snake track."

Bruce motioned toward the cigar ash. "He might have killed Catherwood himself."

"Shore. I thought o' thet. He'll git shet o' the kid, and hog it all. But what fer does he want us?"

"It's one way to watch me. He can rub us out when he's done with us. Or we might be hostages if the Dragoons give him trouble." Bruce rose and, moving to the fireplace, filled his pipe. "Didn't you say Glover wanted you to go with them before Catherwood was killed?" he asked slowly.

"Did so."

"But if Catherwood knew the trail, why would Glover want you?"

"Thet's hit!" Purdy bellowed excitedly. "The varmint asked me 'cause he knowed Catherwood warn't gonna be 'round to do no guidin'. But eff we go with 'em, we won't git to Santy Fee."

"That doesn't count, Bill." Bruce picked up a coal and lighted his pipe. "We've got to keep those guns from going through."

"What's hit to us eff they bust off from Mexico?"

"It's my guess Kearny will be in Santa Fé before winter. Armijo can be bought, but a republic with some Americans running it would be tough to handle, and Kearny's force is small. Besides, some of those guns may be headed for the Comanches."

Purdy swore. "Thet'd be hell for sartain."

"I've got to go to Fort Leavenworth today. I'll meet you at Council Grove, or on the trail between here and there. You help Glover get started. Tell him I had business that took me out of town, but don't tell him where I'm going."

"I'll tell him," Purdy promised, "but eff thet varmint calls me a liar ag'in, I'll make wolf meat out o' him afore he ever gits out clear o' Independence."

IV

Bruce saddled the roan gelding he'd stabled in Independence before he'd gone East for the winter. The horse, Blue Thunder, was a leggy animal with the speed and bottom that a plainsman needed. He was a buffalo horse, and, as Purdy said about his own paint, he could "smell Injun like a beaver smells bait."

Carrying his Hawkins rifle crosswise in front of him, Bruce left town, the uneasy feeling raveling down his spine that he had been watched from the moment he had left

Aunt Sukey's place. But it was not till he had reached the trail that angled along the bluffs bordering the Missouri that he looked back, and saw Mick Catherwood riding after him.

Bruce pulled up and dismounted. He could guess what was in the boy's mind, and this was as good a time as any to have it out. He waited, rifle in his hands, until Mick reined his lathered, mud-splattered horse to a stop.

"Climb down and get it off your chest," Bruce said coldly.

"I aim to." Mick stepped down, hand on his pistol. "I figured you'd try to run out. I should have killed you yesterday, but I had to listen to Purdy and be fool enough to believe what you said about bringing in the killer."

"I'm not running out. Glover signed me and Purdy to guide your train. I'll meet the outfit in Council Grove as soon as I get back."

"You'll never come back!" Mick cried fiercely, drawing a gun. "I aim to fix it so you won't be able to."

Bruce had heard about Ed Catherwood and this boy, how the mother had been killed in a Comanche attack years before when the trader's first caravan was bound for Santa Fé. There had been a closeness between Catherwood and Mick that had become almost a legend on the frontier. Now the boy was out of his mind with grief, and Bruce could see how it was with him. But he couldn't stand here and let the kid shoot him down. Mick was slowly bringing his pistol up, steeling himself to do this killing job that he thought had to be done.

"I think Curt Glover killed your father," Bruce said. His words brought a shadow of indecision to Mick's fine-featured face, a moment of hesitation in the lift of the gun, a moment long enough for Bruce to swing the barrel of his rifle at the kid's head.

Mick's pistol went off, a wild shot that sang high over Bruce's head. Then he had the kid by the shoulder, and was swinging him around. Immediately his hand fell away, for it had come across the boy's chest, and surprise at his discovery paralyzed him. *Mick Catherwood was a woman!*

Bruce's hand had knocked the coonskin cap from Mick's head. Auburn hair cascaded down her shoulders, and fear flamed in her blue eyes as she plunged away from him.

"I won't hurt you."

"I know you won't," she cried, a hand clutching her knife. "I'll get more than

42

buckskin this time if you move out of your tracks. Or if you ever tell anybody what you've found out."

"You're saying nobody knows you're a woman?" Bruce asked incredulously.

"Curt Glover. No one else. Dad wanted a son, so he made a boy out of me. It's the only way I could be safe on the trail with the kind of men we had around us."

"You're not going to Santa Fé?"

"Certainly," she said, as if no other course had ever entered her mind. "Half the business is mine, and Dad would want me to run it."

Mick Catherwood was very much a woman with her hair shiny bright under the morning sun. She had seemed small and fine-featured for a boy, but now she was exactly as she should be, and Bruce smiled in appreciation when he thought of her in a dress.

"What are you smirking about?" she demanded.

"I was putting a dress on you."

"You can take it off," she blazed. "I'll run the Catherwood half of the business as a man would run it. Don't think. . . ." She paused, lips tightening as she remembered what Bruce had said. "Why did you tell me you thought Glover had killed Dad?"

"Maybe because he smokes cigars."

"Of all the. . . ."

"Did your dad believe in separating New Mexico and making an independent republic?"

"No. He was trying to stop it. Glover was the one who was working with Wade Flint and Pancho Lopez."

"That's right strange," Bruce murmured. "Glover told me and Purdy the opposite."

"You're lying again," she challenged.

"Ask Purdy." He gestured wearily. "Ma'am, this is the biggest year the United States has had since we fought the British and signed the treaty of Ghent. Inside of a month we may be fighting both Mexico and England. The War Department knows that Catherwood and Glover ordered a large shipment of guns and powder, and if they get to. . . ."

"That's another lie," she said hotly. "Dad never took any more guns than we needed to fight off Indian attacks."

"How many wagons have you usually taken?"

"Fifteen."

"This time there are twenty-five."

"That's wrong. We're using the same. . . ." The girl paused, biting a lip as if a new thought had come to her. "Dad went to the

44

mule market yesterday and was going to stay all day. Then he got into an argument with Glover, and I thought they were going to have a fight. He told me to stay and buy ten more mules. He went with Glover, and that was the last time I saw him alive."

"Have they had trouble?"

"They've quarreled from the moment Glover showed up in Independence with Flint. He was supposed to stay in Santa Fé, and Dad didn't know he was coming East until he rode in."

"What about Flint?"

"He was in Santa Fé all last summer and fall trying to organize a revolution against Armijo. The only wealthy Mexican who's with him is Lopez, but there are a number of Americans like Glover who want it to go through."

"Then your father and Glover may have had a ruckus over this separatist movement. Or maybe your dad wouldn't stand for the shipment of guns."

"Glover isn't a murderer, Shane. He's a smart trader, but he doesn't like violence. He's even afraid of the trail."

"Mick, I hope you'll believe I want the man who murdered your father."

"You haven't proved to me you didn't," she flung at him.

"Then think of what four thousand guns distributed among the Comanches will do. Or among the Pueblos and renegades who are in with Flint. Or suppose Armijo gets his hands on them for his soldiers?"

"I know," she said tonelessly. "Before we left Santa Fé, we had reasonable proof that the Comanches had been bribed to attack American caravans bound for Santa Fé."

"The War Department had a high regard for your father," he pressed. "That's the reason for me being sent here. If it had been a traitor or a Mexican, we would have known what to do, but it didn't make sense for your father to be in it. Now he's dead, and I didn't get a chance to talk to him about it. That puts it up to you."

For a time she held her silence, staring westward at the rolling country over which they would soon be traveling. Then she brought her gaze to him, and he sensed the enormous struggle that was going on within her.

"What do you want me to do?" she asked.

"Don't tell anybody what I've told you. Give me your co-operation when I need it. I hope you'll take my word that I had nothing to do with your father's death, and that before we get to Santa Fé I'll have the killer."

"I won't tell anybody." She picked her cap up from the muddy trail and, putting it on, worked her hair under it. "I'll take your word about Dad when you get the killer."

"This will be the toughest trip a Catherwood caravan ever made. If war breaks out before we get there, it's hard to guess what will happen. It would be better if you stayed in Independence where things are a *little* quieter."

"I'm going to Santa Fé," she said flatly.

"If Glover murdered your father, he'd murder again for the other half of the business."

She stepped into the saddle. "I can take care of myself, Shane. By all the laws of justice I should have been a man. I am a man by instinct. I've lifted hair and I'll put my shooting up against yours. If Curt Glover tries to rub me out, he'll find six inches of steel in his belly."

She turned her horse, and he watched her go, knowing he could do or say nothing more. She reined up when she was a dozen paces from him, and flung back: "If you tell anybody I'm a woman, you'll taste that six inches of steel yourself."

"I'll hold my tongue if you hold yours," he said angrily, "which is something most women can't do."

"Don't call me a woman!" she cried, and rode on.

Bruce kept his eyes on her until she disappeared along the trail. She rode as if she were part of the horse, as if she belonged there as she belonged in the sunlight with the untamed wind upon her face.

He smiled as he turned to Blue Thunder and swung into the saddle. There would come a day when Mick Catherwood would find she had other instincts than those of a man.

V

It was late afternoon when Bruce Shane reached Fort Leavenworth. Taking from his hat the letter that Secretary of War Marcy had given him in Washington, he handed it to Colonel Stephen Kearny.

Kearny slit the envelope open, scanned the note, and held out his hand. "I've heard of you, Shane. You're the man who was raised with brass buttons on his jacket and who could be running a bank in Richmond, but you'd rather feel the prairie wind on your face."

"Some call me crazy for it," Bruce said soberly.

"It's the way a man looks at it." Kearny

smiled. "Now about these guns."

Bruce told him what had happened since his return to Independence, and what he suspected about Curt Glover and Wade Flint. "I have no way of being sure those guns are in Glover's train," he added, "but I don't see how it could be any other way. Once we roll out, it will be impossible to get word back to you. My notion was for you to stop the train on the trail and make a search."

"I'll send Lieutenant Barstow in the morning. It's my opinion we won't find the guns in Glover's train. I know something about Flint. I doubt if we've had a smarter filibuster since the days of Aaron Burr."

"It's possible the guns are cached along the trail somewhere," Bruce said thoughtfully.

"In which case I'll give Glover a start and send Barstow down the trail after he leaves Council Grove. I advise you not to rejoin the train, Shane. Flint won't miss the next time he tries for your life."

"It's a chance I have to take, Colonel. If Barstow fails to catch the train, or runs into some Pawnees, there would be nothing to stop the delivery of the guns. If I'm there, I'll find some way to stop them."

■ ■ ■ ■

When Lieutenant Barstow returned, he could report nothing better than failure. "We stopped the train the other side of Blue Camp. Flint wasn't with it. Glover was hostile, but he didn't try to keep us from going through the wagons. Just the usual stuff . . . flour, bacon, peas, corn, and the regular merchandise they've hauled over the trail for years."

Bruce gave Kearny a tight-lipped grin. "You were right, but Flint can't hide four thousand guns and the powder and shot they've got in his pocket."

"No," Kearny agreed. "Chances are it's some place between Independence and Santa Fé. Flint's a strange man, Shane. Well educated. Has a fortune that would give him a comfortable living, but he's got notions about being a Santa Fé Cæsar. He'll give us more trouble than Armijo could."

"I'll put out in the morning," Bruce said. "I'll catch the train the other side of the Oregon Junction."

"Better stay and go with Barstow," Kearny urged again.

Bruce shook his head. "I can't do that."

But Glover's train had moved faster than

Bruce had expected. He reached the trail, passed the forks with the signpost reading **Road to Oregon,** and kept on straight ahead into the land of the peaceful tribes.

He did not catch the train that day. He made camp at dusk, cooked supper, and, spreading his buffalo robe, went to sleep. He was on the trail again with the first hint of golden dawn in the east, keeping Blue Thunder at a steady mile-eating clip, and gave thought to his meeting with Mick Catherwood. With her auburn hair done up and wearing a dress, instead of buckskins, she'd find that she did something to men.

He thought, then, of Curt Glover. He remembered the girl had told him Glover knew her identity. Anger stirred in him, for the man's intentions were plain to read. If he had killed Catherwood, and everything Bruce had learned pointed that way, he was spinning a web of his own scheming, working with Flint because it paid him. The Catherwood girl would be handled in his own way when the time was right.

The anger had not died when he sighted the dust cloud ahead. He had more respect for Wade Flint, or even Armadillo Dunn than he did for Curt Glover.

Bruce caught the train as it was making camp. Glover rode toward him, his usually smooth face lined by the pressure of his anger.

"So you want to go to Santa Fé, do you?" Glover raged. "Well, you sure as hell can ride alone. When I hire a man, he obeys orders. I told you we were pulling out the next morning."

"I had business to attend to. I told Purdy to give you a hand. Didn't he?"

"Yeah, but. . . ."

"Then you've got no holler coming, Glover."

"What business was big enough to take you out of Independence?"

"My business is my business," Bruce said curtly.

Glover motioned on down the trail. "Keep riding."

"We'll keep our word, Glover, whether Shane keeps his or not." It was Mick Catherwood.

She had ridden around a wagon, and she sat her saddle with no sign of trail weariness upon her. She did not look at Bruce. He knew she had her own reason for interfering, the suspicion of him still an overpowering motive in her.

"I'll run this train," Glover said violently.

"Dad was a little lax about you," Mick said, palming a gun. "I aim to change that.

I've been over the trail enough times to know that a man of Bruce Shane's caliber is worth twenty of the desert rats you hired."

"Purdy can guide us," Glover said thickly. "Damn it, Mick, I didn't want this man in the first place."

"Purdy will quit if Shane rides on," Mick pointed out.

"Shane set the Dragoons onto us!" Glover exploded. "He's been to Fort Leavenworth and. . . ."

"How do you know?" Bruce asked.

"I'm guessing, and I don't hear you denying it."

"Have you got anything on this train you were afraid the Dragoons would find?" Mick demanded.

"No, but. . . ."

"All right. It doesn't make any difference if he did go to Fort Leavenworth. Shane's taking us through."

Mick wheeled her horse and rode back around the wagon. For a moment Glover's hazel eyes locked with Bruce's gray ones. There was more than anger in them, Bruce thought. Perhaps fear. Bruce was remembering Mick had said the big man was afraid of the trail. He had tackled something too big for him, and now he felt failure closing in upon him.

"You heard the kid," Glover muttered vehemently and he let it go at that.

Bill Purdy rode into camp an hour later and grinned broadly when he saw Bruce. "How thar, Shane!" he called. "Figgered you rode off to the Blackfoot kentry."

"I like my hair too well."

The mountain man dismounted. "Glover was shore mad enough to grow ha'r on thet bald haid of his'n when the Dragoons stopped us," Purdy said, lowering his voice. "They didn't find nuthin', but he was as scairt as a jack rabbit in front of a coyote."

"Where's Flint?"

"Ain't seen him since we rolled out." Purdy tongued his quid to the other side of his mouth. "Looks like we lost hoss 'n' beaver."

"We'll find them. There's fifteen wagons here, and Glover told us we'd have twenty-five. When we find the other ten, Bill, I've got a notion we'll find the guns we're after and Wade Flint to boot."

They watered stock with the first hint of dawn, cooked breakfast, and harnessed up. There was unnecessary waste of time before the train strung out, men running around hunting articles that had been scattered about, pulling balky mules into place, yell-

54

ing and cursing because their own stupidity and inexperience made things go wrong.

A green outfit, Bruce saw, not yet trail wise. The mules were good animals, the wagons the biggest Conestogas that could be bought. Some of the men were experienced, but many were not — river men, Mexicans, or renegades who would have looked better behind bars than on the trail.

"Is this the kind of men your father used?" Bruce asked Mick.

"No," she answered. "Glover hired these. Said he had to take what he could get." Looking back, she saw that Glover was out of earshot. "Wade Flint and ten wagons are waiting in Council Grove. They may be the wagons your Dragoons were looking for."

Bruce nodded gloomily. Stephen Kearny had been right. Flint was playing it the safest way he could. Once the Dragoons had had their look, Glover had figured they were not likely to be back for another. Flint had counted on Bruce's doing the very thing he had.

"Glover was nearly crazy when the Dragoons were searching the wagons," Mick went on. "I never saw him so excited. I think he's beginning to see what will happen if he fails. He'd like to get out, but he doesn't know how."

"How did he explain the ten extra wagons to you?"

"He had a little trouble." She laughed. "I've learned more about Curt Glover since we left Independence than in all the time I'd known him before. He wants it all, but he doesn't have enough courage to play for high stakes." She gave Bruce a straight look. "It takes a certain kind of person to drive a knife into a man's back when he isn't looking. Glover isn't the kind."

"You think I am?"

She looked away then, and took a moment to answer. "No," she admitted finally, "and that leaves me hanging like a green scalp in a Comanche lodge."

They rolled into Council Grove late the following afternoon. Here were water and shade. Both were welcome. More than 100 wagons were scattered in the grove, most of them belonging to emigrants who believed that Kearny would annex New Mexico when war broke out and were anxious to get there ahead of the rush so they could have their pick of home sites.

It was a scene that never failed to amuse Bruce when he saw it. Men were mending harness, gathering firewood, chopping down trees, greasing wheel hubs. Women were washing, bending over cook fires, sewing. This was the last jumping-off place. Ahead was buffalo country, and, where there were buffalo, there would be Indians: Pawnees, Arapahoes, Kiowas, Cheyennes, and the terror of every caravan, the Comanches.

Glover led the train on through the grove to the far end where Flint waited with the other wagons. Bruce, scanning the people who were making their final preparations here, was sobered by what he saw. Many were woefully unprepared for what lay ahead. There were vehicles of all sort, some of them decrepit farm wagons that would never get as far as the Little Arkansas. Many lacked sufficient stock to replace the ones that would die in harness.

"Wolf meat they'll be," Purdy muttered.

A baby tottered away from a wagon and fell and began to cry. Mick looked at the sight, her mouth twitching. "Fools," she whispered. "They should have stayed in town." Turning in her saddle, she watched the baby until its mother picked it up. Again Bruce smiled when he thought of her boast that she had a man's instinct.

"We'll lay over a couple of days, Shane, and see that everything is in good shape," Glover said when Bruce swung out of the saddle.

"From here on it's your job to keep things moving."

"You've got some damned poor men," Bruce said bluntly. "Act like they don't know which end of a mule goes frontward."

"You teach 'em." Glover winked at Flint, apparently in better humor than when Bruce had caught the train. "Part of your job, Shane."

"I came in a day or so ago with this other bunch of wagons," Flint said in his soft, courteous voice. "They seemed competent."

Bruce followed Flint's gesture with his eyes. Most of the men were playing cards on the ground. Some were working on the wagons or repairing harness. They were veterans of the trail, tough and confident.

"They'll do," Bruce said, pondering this thing he'd seen.

"I believe we met in Mogan's Saloon." Flint's smile went no farther than his lips. "I'm with this caravan as a passenger, but I'll do my share of the fighting if it comes to that. I trust there will be no ill feeling from our little disagreement in Mogan's Saloon."

"Not if you follow orders."

"Then we'll get along." Nodding, Flint turned away.

"Bruce, you heerd?" Purdy bawled, coming in a stiff-legged lope from the emigrants' wagons. "We got war with Mexico jest like I figgered. We'll lose hoss 'n' beaver soon as we show up in Santy Fee."

"War?" Glover whispered the word. "How in hell do you know, Purdy?"

"Some coot jest rode in from Independence. He's got a Saint Louis *Republican.*"

"That's right." Mick had come up behind Purdy, her gaze touching Bruce's face. "It says that Captain Thornton of the Dragoons had been attacked and his command captured."

"And Zach Taylor's sitsheashun is ex . . . ex . . . ," Purdy began.

"Extremely perilous," Mick prompted.

"And he's in a hell of a fix," Purdy added.

Glover took off his hat and wiped his baldhead. He turned to Flint who had come to stand beside him. "You hear?"

"I heard, but I doubt if it will affect us," Flint said smoothly. "Taylor is a long ways from Santa Fé. However, it may be well to hurry our plans."

"We'll roll in the morning, Shane," Glover ordered tersely.

"You said we'd lay over," Bruce reminded him. "Some of your greenhorns will need a few days to get acquainted with their mules."

"They can get acquainted on the trail. I said we'd roll in the morning."

"Then I reckon we'll roll," Bruce agreed mildly.

Ordinarily caravans laid over in Council Grove to organize and make whatever repairs were necessary before starting into Indian county. Kearny would figure on that, timing Barstow's departure from the fort accordingly. If Glover kept the pace he'd set so far — and his mules were good enough to do that — Kearny's Dragoons would never catch the train this side of Cimarron Crossing.

There was no way to inform Kearny except to ride back to Fort Leavenworth, and he'd bring on a showdown if he tried that. Later, when the wagoners learned what Flint was doing, they might be led against him.

Tonight they'd follow him. Even if Bruce did go back to the fort, it was not likely he could get there in time. Before he could return to Council Grove with the Dragoons, the caravan would be miles along the trail to Santa Fe.

"I wonder what our guide is thinking about," Flint murmured.

"If he's thinking about heading back to Fort Leavenworth," Glover grated, "I'll sure as hell shoot him before he gets out of the Grove."

"Maybe you'd like to start shooting now?" Bruce challenged.

"And foller your nose across the *Jornada*," Purdy added.

"I meant I didn't want you running out," Glover said. He strode away with Flint following.

Purdy's somber gaze followed them. "Wa-al, son, looks like hit's you 'n' me."

VI

Bruce called the men together that night. "Some of you have been over the trail," he said. "You know the importance of obeying orders, of taking your turns at guard duty, and not riding away from the train to hunt or see the country. We'll have discipline in this train" — his eyes swung to Glover and Flint — "or there'll be wolf meat along the trail. We'll move in columns of four when possible and necessary. When corralling from that formation, the outside columns will wheel together in front, the others swinging out. That'll give us a hollow square, wagon tongue to tail gate. It'll give us a place to hold our stock after grazing and a place to hole up when we smell In-juns."

A group of emigrants had joined the circle of men. One said: "We'd like to travel with you, Shane. We've got nigh onto a hundred wagons, but we ain't got a plainsman in our outfit."

"Curt Glover owns this train." Bruce motioned to him. "That'd be up to him to say."

"I say no," Glover snapped. "We ain't nursing no bunch of greenhorns. If you don't have a plainsman, go back to Independence."

"We'll take our chances if we have to," the man said stubbornly, "but we heard you had two guides. If we could have one. . . ."

"I think not," Flint cut in. "Glover is paying both men high wages. We need Purdy because Shane hasn't been over the *Jornada.*"

It was the first time Flint had dispelled the fiction that Glover was giving the orders. The trader threw a straight glance at him, anger sparking his eyes, but he kept his silence. The emigrants moved disconsolately back to their own wagons, muttering about the damned stubborn traders.

"You got anything to say?" Bruce asked Glover.

"No."

"I have." Flint's enigmatic smile was showing at the corners of his mouth. "The question of whether we lose our hair depends on the speed we make. It is our intention to make a record for travel on the trail. If we don't, we may not find Santa Fé receptive to our entrance."

Bruce had noted that the men who had brought the ten wagons were gathered on one side of the fire. Flint had addressed his words to these men.

"All right," Flint said. "We'll get all the sleep we can."

Circling the fire, Bruce caught Flint and Glover before they left. He asked bluntly: "Let's settle one thing now. Are we two outfits or one?"

"We're one," Flint said in his soft voice.

Glover muttered — "That's right." — and stomped away.

Flint stood there for a moment, black eyes locked with Bruce's, his bland inscrutable face giving no sign of what was in his mind.

"I hope everybody remembers that," Bruce said.

"We will," Flint promised.

When he had gone, Bill Purdy spat into the fire. "Hell of a passel of green scalps in this outfit ready to be lifted, son."

They hitched up when dawn was no more than a golden promise in the east. The mules had been rounded up and watered, the loose stock gathered behind the wagons. There were these moments of chaos of plunging horses and kicking mules, of men's curses and angry yells.

Bruce, riding Blue Thunder, called: "Catch up! Catch up!"

More cursing and yells of pain when a kicking mule hit his target and harness jangle. Then a wagoner yelled: "All set!" Another echoed it: "All set!" The cry ran along the line. "Stretch out!"

There was the *crack* of whips, the *creak* of heavily loaded wagons.

"Fall in!" Bruce bellowed above the clamor.

The train strung out along the western slope toward the highland, Bruce and Bill Purdy at the head. The last jumping-off place! The sunrise behind them. Indian country ahead. And beyond was Santa Fé in an enemy province with Manuel Armijo slouched at his desk in the adobe Governors' Palace.

Riding along the line of wagons to the front was Flint Wade, still smiling, still courteous, his thoughts deep and secret things behind his black expressionless eyes.

In distant Fort Leavenworth Colonel Stephen Kearny had no way of knowing that the caravan, loaded with weapons for the inchoate Republic of New Mexico, was on the march.

The grass came high on the legs of the horsemen. Wind from the distant Rockies touched their faces. The sun beat down with a dry, staggering heat. And wolves prowled hopefully in the distance.

Mick Catherwood joined them. Bruce, watching Flint, saw the break in the man's composure, saw the mask replaced, but that second-long wash of passion had been enough. Flint knew that Mick was a woman, that if he could enlist her aid, she could furnish the flesh and blood he needed to give life to the skeleton of his scheming, and another worry was born to plague Bruce Shane.

The caravan became trail wise in the days that followed, partly because inexperienced men learned by necessity, but mostly because Bruce had the plains savvy and an innate sense of leadership that made men respect him. This was his talent, his choice of life.

Bill Purdy wagged his grizzled head, and muttered: "Book larnin' didn't faze him. Takes to this like a Comanche takes to ha'r." Neither Glover nor Flint interfered. Even Mick Catherwood looked at Bruce with an unconscious respect in her blue eyes.

The miles dropped behind as the wagon train rolled toward the sunset. Diamond Spring. Cottonwood Creek. On to the crossing of the Little Arkansas, steep-banked and treacherous. They swept across it, the lumbering wagons swaying and twisting like white-sailed vessels in a high wind, the water churned into a brown foam.

On into the buffalo country, the lush grass behind, the low-growing nutritious buffalo grass around them. Into the land claimed by the Pawnees.

Bruce, riding ahead with Mick Catherwood, sighted the Arkansas. A great river heading in the high Rockies far to the west, stinking and muddy here, wide of bottom, cluttered with brush and cottonwoods, and, in spots, treacherous with quicksand. Here were wildflowers and dust, prairie dogs and jack rabbits and wolves, a hammering sun and water hardly drinkable and wind that scoured their faces with sand. They had traveled fast, faster than Bruce had expected, but here they stopped, for Purdy had brought word that buffalo were just ahead.

There was meat the next day, hump steak and tenderloin and marrow, meat eaten nearly raw, blood running down men's beards, greasy hands wiped on buckskins, bones gnawed clean. They ate until bellies were stuffed, and then slept, forgetting the danger of Indian attack for the moment.

Bruce watched the first half of the night, Purdy the second. A moon climbed into a clear high sky, and stars made a swath of light above. Wolves prowled around the wagon circle, eyes emerald gems in the thin light.

There was a wildness in this land, a wildness that centuries of Indian occupation had not changed. It was here in the great emptiness, in the night breeze, in the presence of the wolves. Bruce Shane, moving silently around the wagons, ears keening the wind, was conscious of it, and stirred by it as he always was when he left human settlement far behind.

Suddenly Mick Catherwood was beside him. "I couldn't sleep for the snoring," she said. "They're as drunk as if they'd cracked a barrel of Taos lightning."

Bruce leaned his Hawkins rifle against a wagon wheel. "Walnut creek ahead. Pawnee Rock. Ash Creek. Pawnee Forks. Then Cimarron Crossing. That'll be the last chance to stop Flint. Once he gets his wagons across the *Jornada,* they'll go on to Santa Fé, and all hell won't stop 'em."

"What are you going to do?"

"I don't know yet. The Dragoons are behind us, but they won't get here in time."

"Glover is sick of his bargain with Flint," she said. "I finally pried the whole thing out of him. Flint knew him in New York when he was in trouble of some kind. He didn't say what it was, but he was working in a bank, so I guess he'd stolen some money. Anyhow, Flint was going to tell Dad if Glover didn't throw in with him. He promised Glover that, when the new republic was set up, he'd give him a monopoly on all the trail trade. So Glover ordered the guns without Dad knowing anything about it."

"Whose wagons are the ones that were waiting for us in Council Glove?"

"Flint's. He hired those men, but I don't think they know what they're hauling." She looked up at him, her head turned so that the moonlight was fully upon her face. "I keep thinking about what you said that day you left Independence for Fort Leavenworth, about it being up to me now that Dad's gone. I'll be beside you and Bill Purdy when you call for the showdown."

"Thanks, Mick."

VII

It was the first time he had felt she fully trusted him. She could shoot as well as he could. She had brought down her buffalo that morning. He knew she could have split his heart the day her father was murdered. But those were men's talents, and Mick Catherwood was a woman.

"You must have some other name than Mick," he said softly.

"Dad gave me that name." She was close to him, lips upturned. "I was christened Marian."

He knew she had read his mind. Something had happened back along the trail, something she probably did not fully understand herself.

"You're not a man," he said a little roughly. "It's time you stopped thinking you were."

"I thought you were the man who'd stop me thinking it."

Her words were an invitation, and he did not need a second. He kissed her, holding her hard slim body against his.

She was limp for a moment, and then fire swept through her and she was giving his kiss back, fiercely, compellingly, as if she had discovered something that she had not known was in the world.

He let her go.

"You see how it is, Marian. You've played you're man, but there's something in you that won't let you keep on playing that way."

She did not move for a long time. He heard her breathe, rapidly as if she was still riding a high wave of emotion. Then she whispered: "So that's all it is to you." Wheeling, she ran from him.

He understood, then, what he'd done and what he'd lost.

They crossed Walnut Creek the next day. Then Pawnee Rock loomed ahead, a yellow sandstone cliff ominously shadowing the trail, and tension built until men's nerves were ready to snap, for all of them knew that this was the bloodiest point between Independence and Santa Fé.

On to Ash Creek. Glancing back, Bruce saw smoke pillars rise from the frowning top of the rock. He hurried the wagons across the creek, and they made a tight corral, but there was no attack that night.

"Passin' the word on to thar brothers," Purdy said. "We'll hear more of 'em when we git down the trail a piece."

"Too many of us," Glover said with false confidence. "They took a look and saw we were too strong."

Bruce didn't tell the man how wrong he was. Curt Glover was like a boy whistling at night in a graveyard. Bruce understood him better after what Mick had told him. A weak and cowardly man, but he might still be the means of keeping the guns from going through.

They crossed Pawnee Fork and angled southward with the river. That morning Wade Flint rode beside Bruce at the head of the train. Purdy was scouting ahead of the caravan, and Glover and Mick were somewhere behind with the wagons.

"I wonder if you've heard the rumor," Flint said in his soft voice, "that a great many British army officers were hunting Independence this spring. Or, as some said, to enjoy our scenery."

"I heard it," Bruce said. "It may be a big year for the United States, Flint."

Flint nodded bland agreement. "It may also be a year when we put an end to this idea that the continent belongs to those who sit in the seats of the mighty in Washington."

"You're wrong," Bruce challenged. "Traitors will hang now as they have hanged before. We've got a war with Mexico, and Kearny will occupy Santa Fé. Frémont is in California. The Stars and Stripes will fly on the shores of the Pacific before the year is out, Flint."

Flint met Bruce's eyes, the strange smile on his lips. "It's too big a country to rule that way, a fact you well know, Shane. A few of Benton's ilk talk about expansion. The solid men like Daniel Webster realize the facts of geography. There will be an Anglo-Saxon republic in New Mexico, another on the Pacific coast. They will not be drains on the United States, and their people will be ruled more justly than they could be by officials in Washington who think the country ends at the Mississippi."

"Look, Flint." Bruce turned in his saddle, pinning his gaze on the man. "Let's stop trying to fool each other. You know why I'm here, so you had Armadillo Dunn make a try for me in Mogan's Saloon. You tried to nail down my hide for Ed Catherwood's murder. You hired Snake River Joe to bore me on the street. Your luck was bad, so you figured the safest way to handle me was to hire me to guide the train so you could watch me. When you were done with me, you could shoot me in the back and let the wolves gnaw my bones."

"You're a smart man," Flint said amiably. "Through certain connections that I have in Washington, I was informed why you returned to Independence when you did. I'm not sorry now that my plans for you failed. I've come to appreciate your talents. We can't fail, Shane. Armijo will run without firing a shot. Kearny's Dragoons have neither the supplies nor the numbers to force a way through Raton Pass. It will be late this fall before he even gets to Fort Bent. By that time the British will be at war with the United States. The Republic of New Mexico will be a fact. A man with your ability could go far. . . ."

"You can stop right there," Bruce choked, the muzzle of his rifle swinging to cover Flint. "I'll see you fry in your own fat if I have to throw you into the pan myself."

Flint laughed. "When you left the Dragoons at Fort Leavenworth, my friend, you signed your own death warrant. Unless, of course, you're smart enough to throw in with us and obviously you're not." He motioned back along the train. "I pay the men well that I hired. Glover is a weak thing, but he'll go with us and bring his men. It's you and Purdy against my fifty. The odds will be longer after we cross the Arkansas. I've made a deal with the Comanches to see that we get through."

Wade Flint was talking straight. Bragging in his own self-centered way. Bruce read him as a dangerous, frustrated man, intense and inward-looking, determined to play Cæsar in Santa Fé as Kearny had said. He'd fail as ingloriously as Aaron Burr had failed, but, unless it could be handled here, he'd flood this parched land with a river of blood such as it had never known under Spanish rule.

So Bruce held his temper and lowered his rifle, sensing that this wasn't the time. Somehow Flint's men had to be cut away from him. "Looks like we've lost hoss and beaver," he said at last, and turned his eyes ahead.

"I'm glad you recognize that, Shane. One more thing. I know that Mick Catherwood is a woman. If you play my way, I'll see that she isn't hurt. If you don't, she goes to the Comanches."

"All right," Bruce said thickly, and spurred ahead, anger a volcanic force in him.

He had underestimated Wade Flint, misjudged his cruelty, his passion for power, his ruthlessness. Bruce knew now he loved Mick Catherwood, knew that if they lived, their destinies would be one here in this new raw land.

He found her that night, and told her what Flint had said.

"It's in the open now," he said bitterly,

"but if I wind up being wolf meat, I aim to take Flint with me. I get that far in my thinking. Then I remember that, if something goes wrong, the Comanches will get their hands on you, and then I can't think at all. Before we get to the Cimarron Crossing, you've got to light out for Bent's Fort."

The red glow of the fire was on her face, the strong tanned face of one who knows the savagery of this land and counts the risk as part of the day's work. There was something else in her face, too, the look of a woman who has discovered she possesses something she thought had been lost.

"I'll play it out, Bruce," she said simply. "Perhaps our scalps will hang in the same Comanche lodge."

His grin was tight-lipped and mirthless. "A fine future," he said, knowing he had expected no other answer.

The train rolled westward and tension grew until men's tempers snapped for no reason at all. They were being watched and their progress reported by smoke talk, but the red devils stayed out of sight. Stock was grazed under double guard and then driven into the hollow square. Saddle horses were kept on short rope pickets beside men as they slept restlessly, waiting for the attack.

Curt Glover kept his dignity, but he

mopped his baldhead often, and sometimes his hazel eyes held doubt as they turned to Bruce Shane. The caravan reached The Caches, the Cimarron Crossing just ahead, and Bruce had an opportunity to talk to Glover alone.

"You've got fifteen wagons loaded with legitimate merchandise," he said bluntly. "You let Flint throw in with you because you're afraid of him and because he made you a promise he'll never keep. The minute he rides into Santa Fé, he'll be done with you, and he'll cut your heart out."

"I don't know what you're talking about," Glover snarled.

"You know all right. If you're still alive when Kearny marches into Santa Fé, you'll have a rope around your neck. It'll be Flint and his hired guns against Kearny's Dragoons. Even if Flint doesn't slit your gullet, you're smart enough to know that in the long run Flint can't win."

Glover wiped a film of sweat from his forehead. "Go to hell," he said thickly.

"You'll have a chance to save your hide!" Bruce called. "If you aren't man enough to take it, you can count on that neck stretching."

The Caches fell behind. The air was hot and heavy and without motion, the sky a sullen steel-gray. Lightning lanced the western horizon. Then they reached the Crossing and corralled. Bruce splashed through the water to scout among the sand-hills and Purdy rode upstream while Flint chafed at the delay.

"We'll have no trouble with the Comanches," he told Glover. "I say to cross today and to hell with Shane."

"We'll wait," Mick said tersely. "We're taking Shane's orders in case you've forgotten the agreement."

"We'd have a hell of time getting across the *Jornada* without Purdy," Glover added.

"It may be we won't need a guide," Flint said, but he didn't press the argument.

Bruce and Purdy were back in camp before dark.

"Cain't see nuthin' ahaid," Purdy told Glover, "but they ain't quit watchin' us. Thar's a million brownskins jest out o' sight, or this 'coon cain't tell pore bull from fat cow."

"Plenty on the other side," Bruce said. "We'd better go the long way."

"We're going the dry route," Flint snapped.

"What about it, Glover?" Bruce asked.

The trader shifted uncomfortably and fumbled for a cigar. For a moment Bruce thought he'd take a stand against Flint. But Flint's influence on the big man was greater than his fear of the Indians or the rope Bruce had promised him.

"We left Independence planning on crossing the *Jornada,*" Glover said. "I don't see any reason for changing things now. Fact is, Shane, that's why we hired Purdy."

"Then we cross in the morning," Bruce said, "if we've still got our hair."

The sun dropped from sight and a black oppressive sky crowded the earth. There was no wind; heat lay upon them like a sticky blanket. Bruce moved inside the wagon circle, ordering the fires out and telling every man to look to his gun.

"They won't attack till dawn," he told them. "Maybe not then. Might let us get halfway across the *Jornada* before we see 'em."

When Bruce completed the circle to where he had picketed Blue Thunder, Mick Catherwood was waiting for him. "Comanches?" she asked. "I noticed you didn't say."

"Kiowas. A lot of 'em. Maybe we can beat 'em off, but if we get into the *Jornada,* we're gone beaver." When he reached for her and brought her to him, she did not pull away from his grip. "I've got to tell you or I may never get another chance. I love you. When we get to Santa Fé, I'm going to ask you to marry me."

She was in his arms, her lips meeting his, and there was this moment when terror and fear and shadow were not of this world. Then she drew away. "We've had at least one fight every trip we've made, and I still have my hair. We'll make it this time, Bruce."

Slipping away, she disappeared into the darkness. He smiled grimly, knowing better than anyone else how slim their chances were. This spring of 1846 was like no other year.

They wore out the long hours, none sleeping. Bruce made his rounds, lifting sagging spirits. Then, near dawn, Bill Purdy said: "We're in fer hit, son. I've got a feelin'. Jest like I can allus tell hit's gonna rain when thet damned arrerhaid in my ribs begins to ache."

Curt Glover lying under the next wagon said: "We haven't seen a redskin since we left Council Grove. I don't know why. . . ."

"Flint! You there, Flint?" It was a rumbling voice from near the river. For a pregnant moment no one answered. There was not even a whisper inside the enclosure. Then Bill Purdy rapped out an oath. "Thet's

79

Armadillo Dunn. I'd know his voice in hell. We're gone beaver eff he gits his brownskins inside."

"Dunn." The word, a choked curse from Curt Glover's dry tongue, was echoed on around the wagon circle.

Knowing the depths of Dunn's duplicity, Bruce thought he recognized the renegade's game. Dunn would not know what decision had been made about going the long way by Fort Bent, or the short trail across the dreaded *Jornada.* It would be Dunn's purpose to persuade them to take the dry route. Then, with the train divided and the river between, he'd signal for the attack.

"Tell him to come in, Flint," Bruce said softly. "Bill, keep your eyes on Flint. Let him talk to Dunn, so we can see what the devil's got on his mind."

"Ain't you there, Flint?" Dunn called again.

"I'm here," Flint answered. "Come in."

Bruce saw the man's bulky shape lift itself from the black earth and come toward the train in a twisting run. He threw himself under a wagon, puffing. "Where are you, Flint?"

"Here. What are you doing on the river?"

"Injuns closin' in," the renegade panted. "I jest came across the *Jornada* from Santy

80

Fee. The Comanches won't bother us, but the Cheyennes will. You've got to get across the river and keep rollin'. Soon as the Comanches find us, we'll be safe because the Cheyennes won't. . . ."

"But it's Kiowas out there," Mick Catherwood cried, "and it was Kiowas that attacked the two other trains you led before!"

"Shet up, kid," Dunn snarled. "I say them brownskins air Cheyennes. I orter know 'cause they nearly got my ha'r."

"But Shane said they were Kiowas," Mick insisted.

"Shane." Dunn whispered the name.

"I'm here all right," Bruce said grimly, coming along the wagon to where Flint and Dunn were. "I told you I'd kill you."

Dunn rose and plunged at Bruce, his knife slashing the air. They came together hard, both knowing this time there would be death for one or the other. There was no exchange of blows. No kicking. No eye gouging.

"Give him Green River," Purdy said.

There was the shuffling of feet in the sand. Grunts from the fighting men. No other sound but the breathing of the watchers. If Flint realized how much was at stake, he gave no sign. Glover pressed against a wagon wheel, face tightly drawn by fear.

81

Mick Catherwood stood nearest to the fighters, her slim hands clenched, a prayer in her heart as she watched.

The renegade's knife inched closer to Bruce's chest. Suddenly, without warning, Bruce released his grip on Dunn's right wrist and bowed his body back. Dunn's knife whipped down like a bowstring suddenly released from tension, the razor-sharp point slashing the front of Bruce's buckskins and opening a long shallow gash. In that same instant Dunn's grip on Bruce's right wrist instinctively relaxed, and Bruce whipped his blade into the renegade's hard-muscled belly and slashed a half circle.

Dunn wilted and fell, blood pouring into the sand. Purdy pounced upon him, crying: "Hyar's wolf meat! They'll gnaw your bones clean and die o' your pizen meanness." He ran his knife around Dunn's head and peeled the scalp back. "Want hit, Flint?" Purdy snarled, throwing the bloody mass at Flint.

Bruce wiped his blade across his thigh as Flint stepped back to let the scalp fall at his feet. He said: "When you deal with a coyote like Dunn, you can expect to get sold out. Kiowas are waiting for us to line out across the river. If we'd done what your man wanted us to, we'd all have lost our hair. I reckon Dunn wanted the gold you're carrying, and his Kiowas wanted your guns and powder. When this is over, Flint, I'll show you how to deal with a traitor if we're both alive." He swung to face the men. "We haven't got long. The devils will expect us to do what Dunn said. When they see we ain't rolling out, they'll tackle us. Fill up the holes with bales and blankets and saddles. Hold your fire till you know you've got a bead on an Injun. We'll save our hair if you don't lose your heads."

They came suddenly, came from where an instant before there had been nothing at all, their yells high and terrifying. Swift moving figures circled the wagons, painted bronze-skinned devils, loosing a cloud of arrows that rapped into the wagons with sickening *thuds.*

Rifles *cracked.* Flame tongues vomited into the dawn light. Purdy's exulting battle cry rose above the din as a Kiowa was knocked off his horse. "Give hit to 'em fer hoss 'n' beaver, boys. Thar's one fer the wolves to chaw."

Mick Catherwood lay beside Bruce under a wagon, her rifle taking the same toll his was exacting.

Men cried out in agony. Kiowas split the air with strident, taunting war cries. Whites flung back their curses. Horses plunged and neighed. Mules brayed.

An arrow ripped into Bruce's shoulder. He clenched his teeth and reloaded his rifle. Outside an Indian crept close to the wagons, raised his bow, and died before the crack of Mick Catherwood's gun.

"We got 'em, boys!" Bill Purdy howled. "They're pulling out."

"They'll hang around waiting for us to roll out," Bruce said, "so we'll fool 'em and stay corralled."

"I'll give the orders now, Shane," Flint said quietly. "We'll roll out now, and I don't want to hear any argument out of you about going the Fort Bent way."

"We're staying here, Flint." Bruce swung a hand toward the men who had begun to gather. "You're Americans, most of you, and being Americans there's only one thing you can do when you're told that Wade Flint is freighting four thousand guns into Santa Fé to supply an army he hopes will establish a Republic of New Mexico, an army that will fight Kearny. Some of these guns are supposed to go to the Comanches who have been bribed to stop every American caravan on the trail. Flint's a traitor."

"You're a fool, Shane, if you. . . ."

"These guns will kill American Dragoons

in Raton Pass," Bruce cut in, "or Apache Cañon. I say to hold them here till Kearny comes, and hold Flint for Kearny to hang."

Bruce couldn't tell, by watching the men, whether he'd convinced them or not. They stood in indecision while Flint's taunting laugh slapped at Bruce.

"I said you were a fool, Shane. I'm paying these men good wages to get these wagons through." He turned to the wagoners. "We've beaten off the redskins once. We can do it again. Harness up and get across. If Shane makes any trouble, put him on his horse and start him for Fort Bent."

They didn't move, still gripped by indecision. It was Curt Glover, under the next wagon with an arrow in his paunch, who made up their minds.

"Shane's right!" Glover shouted. "Flint was inside the wagon while we did the fighting. He killed Ed Catherwood before we left Independence because Catherwood was raising hell about the guns."

Flint wheeled on him. Hand whipping to his gun, he bawled an oath — and then crumpled before the blazing blast of Bruce Shane's pistol.

"Stay corralled till the Dragoons come," Bruce breathed, and, breaking at knee and waist, fell into the sand that was made wet by his blood.

Mick Catherwood cradled his head in her lap. Purdy cried: "We'll push thet arrer through and cut the shaft! Thet boy ain't gonna be wolf meat on the trail."

Bruce's eyes were open, searching the girl's. He whispered: "I gambled that those boys wouldn't back Flint when they knew the truth. That's why he pulled his gun on Glover. If Glover hadn't had his say, I'd have been gone beaver."

"Glover showed more courage than I thought he had in him." Tears were in her eyes. "Bruce, you've got to live."

"Sure. I want to see Kearny march into Santa Fé after I get some marrying done."

And Bill Purdy, knife in hand, had to wait in astonishment while Mick Catherwood kissed Bruce Shane on the lips.

"What the hell . . . ," Purdy began.

"A woman, Bill," Bruce murmured, "who found out that all of her instincts weren't a man's."

■ ■ ■ ■

TWELVE HOURS TILL NOON

■ ■ ■ ■

I

Amity was on the biggest binge in its history, not alcoholic, but one of exuberance and enthusiasm and triumph. Tomorrow was Dam Day. Enough money had been raised to finish building the dam on Buffalo Creek and the main canal as well, so the completion of the irrigation project was insured at last.

As far as Sheriff Jerry Corrigan was concerned, this was fine. In fact, it was strictly wonderful because he could marry Jean Dugan next month as planned. Not that there had been any doubt — except in his own mind. He had worried because the sheriff's salary was pretty slim for supporting a family.

But now all his worries were over, for Corrigan was one of the lucky ones. His quarter-section below town would be under the ditch and so overnight he had become a well-to-do man. Not by any effort on his part. It was just that his place was located in the right spot. Land that had been good only for grazing would now be the most valuable in the country.

The trouble was that Amity had rolled out the red carpet for the celebration tomorrow. In spite of the hot weather that had held for several days, everybody who lived in the county was in town, and it even seemed to Corrigan that most of the people of Colorado were here, too. The hotel was crammed, every spare bedroom had been rented out for the night, and people were camped up and down the creek on both sides of town.

Tomorrow at noon the Populist governor of Colorado, Benjamin Wyatt, would speak. There would be a band concert, a free lunch, and then the land that was for sale and would be irrigated from the proposed Buffalo Creek project would be auctioned off. After that, there would be dancing in the Masonic Hall.

Yes, Corrigan told himself as he prowled Main Street and the side streets and the alleys, this was all very fine. It was stupid to kick good fortune in the face. Still, it was a hell of a thing when you're twenty-five years old and so much in love with your girl that you can't bear to be away from her, but you can't leave your job long enough to take her buggy riding as you had promised.

He was supposed to have picked Jean up hours ago. Yes, supposed to, and then he was supposed to get back to town in time to attend a meeting that Jean's father, Matt Dugan, had called for the committee heads to go over the final plans for the celebration tomorrow.

Matt was the general chairman. Corrigan didn't want to make him sore, but right now he knew he wasn't going to that meeting. If Jean wasn't mad at him, and, if the damned town ever settled down, he was still going to take her buggy riding.

He stepped into the hotel bar and glanced around. The crowd had thinned out and the men who were here seemed peaceful enough. He returned to the street and moved on down to Cassidy's Saloon. It, like the hotel bar, wasn't crowded as it had been all evening, and he guessed that both of them would be empty in another half hour.

The Palace across the street was the only other saloon in Amity. Corrigan hesitated, having a notion to get the buggy and pick up Jean and leave town for an hour. The Palace catered to ranchers and cowboys, and, if they wanted to kill each other off, it would be a good idea.

So far today he had stopped three fist fights and one gunfight and had tossed eight men into jail for disturbing the peace or drunkenness or, as he'd told the last one, just plain orneriness. There hadn't been a farmer or a townsman among them. All had been cowboys.

Then he shrugged and crossed the street. When he pushed through the batwings and glanced at the crowd, he groaned. The place was jumping just as it had been an hour ago. From the buzz of talk, he had an idea these men had no intention of leaving. By the time this crowd went home, Jean would be in bed asleep and maybe never speak to him again.

He saw Uncle Pete Fisher talking to three Owl Creek ranchers at the far end of the bar. He started toward them, surprised that Uncle Pete was here. He was an old man, seventy or over, bent by rheumatism and hard work in his youth. He had been the first to settle in Buffalo Creek valley, his original sod house still standing on the slope north of town. He had been a successful stockman and then a banker, but the Panic of 1893 had cleaned him out less than a year ago.

Now Fisher was a defeated and bitter man who smoked countless cheap cigars and lived off his wife's money. Matt Dugan, who had taken over his bank, felt the old man should have a part in tomorrow's celebration, and had given him the job of planning the activities of Amity's brass band.

"Jerry!" Sam Elliott called from behind the bar.

Corrigan stopped, his gaze still on Fisher and the Owl Creek bunch who were, as usual, drinking too much. He knew them all: Vance Yarnell, Zach Lupton, and Harry Mason. They ran shirt-tail spreads near the head of Owl Creek and raised hell every time they came to town.

Corrigan turned to Elliott who owned the place. "Having any trouble?" he asked.

"Not yet, but you may have some tomorrow." Elliott leaned over the bar and said in a low tone: "Jerry, you ought to listen to those Owl Creek boys. They're talking about shooting the governor tomorrow."

Corrigan groaned. He had enough trouble keeping the peace without having to run herd on a bunch of trigger-happy cowboys who hated the Populist governor. Probably they were merely echoing what Uncle Pete Fisher had been telling them. Fisher blamed the Populists and the governor in particular for losing everything he owned and he had sulked ever since he'd heard that Matt

Dugan had invited Benjamin Wyatt to speak.

"Probably just the whiskey talking," Corrigan said.

"No, it's more than that," Elliott said worriedly. "They sold a jag of steers yesterday, and at today's prices they got next to nothing. They're sore about that, and now they're listening to Uncle Pete's wild talk. Of course, he tells them that Wyatt is to blame for the hard times, and tomorrow they'll have a chance to take it out of his hide."

Corrigan shook his head, feeling as if he had been caught in a great flood and was being carried far away from where he wanted to go. "I'll talk to them," he said, and threaded his way through the crowd to where the Owl Creek men stood listening to Fisher.

The old man was saying: "I tell you that, if Wyatt is re-elected in November, the sovereign state of Colorado will be bankrupt. There will be rioting in the streets of every town from Denver down to little burgs like Amity. Blood will flow to our knees. On the other hand, if Wyatt was to die suddenly between now and election day. . . ."

"I don't want to hear anything about Governor Wyatt dying," Corrigan said. "I'm surprised at you, Uncle Pete. The governor is to be our guest for an hour or two tomorrow. It's our job to treat him as a guest."

Fisher turned slowly and glared at Corrigan. He had a mustache and beard that were black, although his hair and brows had turned white long ago. There were those who were irreverent enough to say he used shoe blacking on his mustache and beard, but no one had the temerity to say this to his face.

"You are a young squirt, Sheriff," Fisher said sullenly. "You haven't seen the things happen that I have. The Populists are no better than Socialists or Anarchists. We built this country, these boys and me and Matt Dugan and some more. We hate like hell to see it destroyed by a bunch of fools and crooks. Wyatt is the biggest crook and fool in the lot."

"Matt is expecting you in the bank, Uncle Pete," Corrigan said.

"Well, I ain't ready to go," Fisher snapped. "I was just educating these boys about the Populists and I ain't finished. Look at what they've already done. Brought about the worst panic in the nation's history. Gave women the right to vote here in Colorado. Women's place is in the home tending to their babies, and not going to the polls and holding office and acting like they want to be men."

"Uncle Pete, if you'll just go to the bank. . . ."

"Damn it, I ain't done!" Fisher bellowed. "The Populists want to abolish the national banks. They want the government to take over the railroads and telegraph. I tell you that, if Wyatt is allowed to live, and the fool voters of this state put him back into office. . . ."

"All right, we know how you feel." Corrigan took the old man's arm. "Let's go over to the bank and see if Matt's got his meeting started."

Fisher tried to break free, but failed. Corrigan pulled him toward the batwings, but he had not taken more than two steps until Vance Yarnell said: "Let's take this snot-nosed sheriff and whittle him down to size. He sure needs a lesson, seeing as he ain't dry behind the ears."

Yarnell lunged at Corrigan who had been watching them and, knowing that this was typical of cowboys who hated any figure of authority, had expected some kind of a move. He let go of Fisher's arm and drove his fist squarely at Yarnell's chin, a pile-driving blow that knocked the Owl Creek man cold. Corrigan jumped back, his gun in his hand.

Lupton and Mason were slow to follow Yarnell's lead, slow enough so that now, facing Corrigan's gun, they lost their appetite for fighting. "Pick Yarnell up," Corrigan ordered. "Tote him out of here. You're going to jail, the three of you."

"You can't do that!" Lupton shouted indignantly. "What'd we do?"

"You attacked an officer of the law," Corrigan said. "Now do what I told you or I'll pistol whip both of you and haul you in myself."

A cowboy on the other side of the room let out a rebel yell and shouted: "Let's take the sheriff's pants off! He's too smart for his britches."

"Stand pat!" Elliott bellowed above the rumble of the crowd as he brought a sawed-off shotgun into view from behind the bar. "Any of you buckos who think you're going to take the sheriff will get your heads shot off. I'll start with you, Holly."

The cowboy who had yelled raised his hands in mock surrender. "I'm sorry, Sam. I decided I don't want the sheriff's pants, after all."

"Get those Owl Creekers out of here, Jerry," Elliott said. "I'm closing for the night."

"Move," Corrigan said.

Cursing, Mason and Lupton picked up Yarnell and started toward the batwings, Corrigan coming behind them, his cocked gun in his hand.

Fisher was already on the boardwalk by the time Corrigan got there with the Owl Creek men. He was meek now as he said: "You're coming to the bank, ain't you?"

"No," Corrigan answered. "I'm supposed to take Jean buggy riding and that's what I'm going to do. You tell Matt that."

"I've got something to tell you," Fisher said, "and you'd better listen. Wyatt will never live to ride out of this town."

Corrigan turned away and went on toward the jail, keeping two paces between him and the Owl Creek men. They reached the end of the business block and crossed the street to the courthouse square. A minute later he locked the three men in a cell, then wheeled and sprinted to the livery stable.

Walt Payson, the liveryman, saw him run through the archway and called: "You don't think Jean is gonna wait up for you this long, do you?"

"I dunno," Corrigan panted. "Just hook that horse up, will you?"

The Dugan house was across the street from the courthouse and directly north of the platform that had been built for the speechmaking and the auctioning of the irrigated land. Corrigan was still breathing hard when he drew up in front of the house and whistled. Usually he walked up the path to the front door and yanked the bell pull, but tonight, as late as he was, he was afraid to. If Jean didn't come, he'd know she'd given up and gone to bed. In that case, he'd take the horse and buggy back to the livery stable and try to see her first thing in the morning.

The front screen slammed shut and he saw her run across the yard to the street. His heart began to pound. He couldn't stand it if she bawled him out. They never had quarreled and he didn't want to start now.

She climbed into the seat beside him, not at all worried because her skirt flew up and exposed her trim ankles. She said: "Lead on, McDuff, or whoever it was I studied in school."

"Honey, I'm sorry I'm late," he said. "I should have been here hours ago, but the town's wild tonight and I couldn't get away."

"And what's more, you probably shouldn't be here now," she said gaily. "Go on. Let's get out of here before you hear somebody shoot somebody else. Find a private little spot of beauty where you can kiss me

99

properly without the neighbors watching us."

"You're not mad at me for being so late?"

"Of course not, silly. I was afraid you couldn't make it at all. Just because you've got red hair and a hot temper aren't reasons for me to get mad at the drop of the hat."

He took a long, sighing breath of relief. "Honey, I love you more every day." He slapped the horse with the lines. "Come on, Napoleon. Haul us out of here."

II

Governor Benjamin Wyatt closed his eyes and relaxed, his head resting against the red plush cloth that covered the back of the seat. He listened absently to the rhythmic *click-click* of wheels on rails as the train thundered eastward across the Colorado plains. They were scheduled to pull into Burlington at midnight and it was nearly that now.

He didn't think he had ever been as tired as he was at this moment, but when you're seventy years old with white hair and a white beard and you look like everybody's grandfather, and when you're making five or more campaign speeches a day, you have a right to feel tired.

He thought about all the things he had tried in his lifetime. He'd been a farmer, a schoolteacher, a soldier during the Civil War, a merchant, a lawyer, and finally a newspaper editor. He had not been outstanding at any of them, and still he had been elected governor of Colorado at the age of sixty-eight on the Populist ticket. It was a sort of miracle any way he looked at it.

Now, with six weeks to go until election day, he wasn't sure how it would turn out, but he thought he had a chance of winning a second term in spite of the panic of the previous year, the vilification, the name calling, and the actual death threats that had been made against him. The women had been given the right to vote during his administration, and he expected their support in return for what he had done for them.

His secretary, Tom Henry, came into the coach from the smoking car and sat down beside him. Wyatt opened his eyes to glance at Henry, then closed them again. Tom Henry was in his middle twenties, a crusader with the drive and zeal of a man who knows the world must be saved and there was very little time left.

Wyatt was always amused when he

thought about this. There had been a time when he had been as young and idealistic as Tom Henry and had been filled with the same zeal and the notion that time was rapidly running out. He had been an Abolitionist; he had even been a conductor on the Underground Railroad. Now, when he was close to the end of his life, he was very much aware that changing the world was a slow process indeed.

"You thought about your speech tomorrow, Governor?" Henry asked.

He patted his beard and sighed. "Yes, I've thought about it. It will, as Matt Dugan suggested, be non-political. I'm sure that if I gave a rousing Populist speech in Amity, I would start a riot."

"I'm afraid you would," Henry said. "You'll have an audience of conservative farmers and ranchers who think any suggestion of change is treason."

"They do," Wyatt agreed. "They do, indeed."

"Are you going to quote from Governor Lewelling's address when he was inaugurated in Kansas?"

"Which quote do you have in mind?" Wyatt asked.

"The best one," Henry said. " 'The people are greater than the law or the statutes, and, when a nation sets forth its heart on doing a great or a good thing, it can find a legal way to do it.' I think that's the way it goes."

Wyatt nodded. "Correct. Yes, I plan to use it. You know, Tom, these Amity people are doing a worthwhile thing and they're doing it themselves. Dugan says they've borrowed the money to build the dam and dig the main canal, and they've already started work. Any of us, Populist or Democrat or Republican, would approve of it."

"Sure," Henry said, "but it gravels me that they asked you to make the speech and then they tell you it has to be non-political."

"They wanted the governor of the state of Colorado," Wyatt said, "and they invited him in spite of his being a Populist. They have land to sell. This will give them free publicity and it will do the same for me."

"But you won't get a damned vote out of it," Henry said hotly. "They may even shoot you before you leave town."

Wyatt smiled. "Oh, come now, Tom. You don't really believe that."

"They might," Henry said doggedly. "You'll have a hostile audience. Even Dugan admitted that."

"Matt Dugan is an honest man for a banker," Wyatt said. "Cussing me and shooting me are two different things. On the other hand, I know some men in Denver, rich men, who would shoot me if they could figure out a way to do it and not get caught. The interesting part of it is that they honestly think they would be saving the state by removing me before I bankrupt it."

Henry swore under his breath. "It doesn't make any sense, Governor. We did not bring on the Panic of 1893, but we get the blame for it."

"I know," Wyatt said wearily. "If I could have persuaded the legislature to give me what I wanted, I could have prevented some of the suffering that took place, but you know what happened."

Henry was silent for a moment, his worried gaze fixed on Wyatt's face, then he burst out: "Governor, you can't go to Amity tomorrow."

Wyatt smiled. "Are we back on that again?"

"Well. . . ." Henry swallowed. "I mean, you're scheduled for a speech in Colorado Springs the day after tomorrow. It's going to be nip and tuck if we make it. We'd better send word. . . ."

"Tom, when did our relationship reach such a low point that you have to lie to me?" Wyatt asked. "You take care of the scheduling. You've done a good job up to now. I find it hard to believe that suddenly you find you've committed a grave error just as we are about to arrive in Burlington."

Henry stared at his hands that were fisted on his lap. "I guess I'm a coward, Governor. I wanted to spare you this and I kept hoping that something would happen that would prevent you from going to Amity in the morning. I guess I'd better show you a letter that came today."

Henry reached into his inside coat pocket and drew out an envelope and handed it to Wyatt who glanced at the address. The words **Tom Henry, Secretary to the Governor, Denver, Colorado,** were printed in pencil. He looked up. "Tom, we've had death threats before, if that's what this is."

"Go on," Henry said. "Look at it."

Wyatt shrugged and took the folded sheet of paper from the envelope. He had always looked upon any death threat as the work of some crackpot who thought he could be scared into withdrawing from the race. He refused to think this was anything else.

The message was printed in pencil on a sheet of cheap tablet paper similar to the kind any child would use in school. Wyatt read: **Plans are complete to murder Governor Wyatt in Amity when he ar-**

rives to speak on Dam Day. It is too late now to call it off, so see that he does not come.

"I know," Henry said when Wyatt looked at him. "I should have showed it to you hours ago, but we were in a hurry to catch the train. I grabbed up several letters just as we left my office and didn't look at them until we were on the train. Then it was like I said. I hoped to spare you this."

"Another crackpot," Wyatt said with feigned indifference.

"I don't think so," Henry said. "For one thing, we know that Amity is one of the centers of hostility to you. The second thing is that I'm guessing someone in Amity helped to make these plans and now he's running scared and hoping it doesn't happen. This was all he could think of doing."

Wyatt handed the envelope back to Henry. "You may be right. In any case, we'll go ahead as planned."

"But damn it. . . ."

The train had begun to slow. Wyatt made an impatient gesture. "Take our bags down, Tom. We're right on time."

Henry, fully aware that Wyatt could be a very stubborn man at times, stepped into the aisle and took their valises from the rack just as the shrill, long drawn-out sound of

106

the whistle came to them.

"We'd better get out there on the platform," Henry said, "and be ready to step off the minute the train stops or we'll wind up in Kansas."

"The Populist vote in Kansas will not elect me in Colorado," Wyatt said as he rose and moved into the aisle.

He followed Henry to the end of the car, the bell *clanging* steadily as he went onto the platform and down the steps where he joined Henry.

The conductor shouted — "B-o-a-r-d!" — and Wyatt saw the lanterns swing and the coach start to move. A moment later smoke from the engine rolled in around them and the bell was sounding again. He remained there on the cinders beside the track until the train was far away, the rear lights growing smaller. The thought came to him that this would be an excellent spot to murder him while he stood in the thin light from the depot lamps.

Wyatt took a handkerchief from his pocket and wiped his face. The night air was hot and without a trace of a breeze. He shrugged his shoulders, telling himself he had never been stampeded into panic by death threats. Still, as Henry had said, this was different. More than that, he was disappointed in

Matt Dugan.

He had never been in Burlington before; he did not know where the hotel was or how far it was from the depot. He had assumed that Dugan would have someone to meet them.

"We'd better start walking," Wyatt said. "I guess we can find a hotel."

"I have a rig to take you to the hotel," a man said as he appeared around the corner of the depot. "Sorry I'm slow getting here. I got into a poker game and the last hand took longer'n I figured. Usually the train's a few minutes late, but it was right on time tonight."

"I suppose a poker game's more important than meeting the governor," Henry said sulkily.

"It's all right, Mister . . . ?" Wyatt began.

"Miles," the man said. "Dick Miles. I work for Matt Dugan."

Wyatt caught the movement of the man's hand in the thin light as he held it out. Wyatt shook it, then said: "Mister Miles, this is my secretary, Tom Henry."

"Howdy, Mister Henry," Miles said, and offered his hand.

Henry put the valises down and grunted something as he shook hands. Wyatt thought he would have to remind his secretary of his manners again. For some reason he always expected the red carpet treatment, which was seldom forthcoming.

"This way," Miles said, and led them around the depot to the hitch rail.

Wyatt took the seat in the hack behind the driver's. Henry dropped the valises in the back and sat down beside the governor.

In less than five minutes they pulled up in front of a hotel, the lights in the lobby and those from a saloon across the street the only signs of life anywhere in the business block.

"They'll have breakfast for us at five," Miles said. "We've got to leave here at least by six if we're going to make it to Amity by noon."

"We'll be ready," Wyatt said.

Henry lifted the valises from the back of the rig and set them on the boardwalk. Miles hesitated, looking down at Wyatt, who sensed he wanted to say something.

"Let's get to bed," Henry said. "I'll see if they have any rooms reserved for us."

"They do and they're paid for." Miles waited until Henry disappeared into the lobby, then he leaned forward. "Governor, there's something I want to say, but Matt will fire me if he knows I said it. He's banking on you being there tomorrow."

"I intend to be there." Wyatt could not see Miles clearly in the dim light from the hotel lobby, but he had the impression of a bronze, strong-jawed man, and, knowing that Matt Dugan was a rancher as well as a banker, he suspected that Miles was a cowhand. He added: "If you can get me there."

"Oh, I can get you there, all right," Miles said, "but I ain't real sure you want to go. What I mean is, you won't get a single, solitary vote out of the bunch that's going to be listening to you tomorrow. It may turn out to be purty unpleasant on account of a lot of people lost their farms and ranches and even some business in town because of the panic last year."

"And of course they blame me and the Populist party."

"They sure do," Miles said. "Now I ain't claiming they're right, mind you, but that's exactly how they feel."

"And some of them hate me enough to take a shot at me," Wyatt said.

"How did you know that?" Miles demanded. "Did anybody tell you?"

"Oh, no," Wyatt said, "but it's an old story. I aim to be in Amity at twelve tomorrow, Mister Miles. Good night."

"Good night, Governor," Miles said, and

drove away. Wyatt turned and went into the lobby, thinking he had lived his three score and ten years and he didn't really care if he lived any longer or not. You never knew what forces pushed a cause toward fulfillment, but sometimes an assassin's bullet did more good than anything else to achieve that fulfillment. If that was his fate, then so be it. Then, for some reason, he wondered if Dick Miles was the man who had sent the death threat to Tom Henry.

III

John Smith and Ross Hart reined up in front of the sod house a few minutes before midnight and dismounted, Smith stiff and sore after the long ride from the Kansas border. He called: "Hello!"

The door was flung open, and lamplight fell past a slim man who stood in the doorway. He asked: "John? Ross?"

"Right," Smith said, and, leaving the reins dragging, stepped into the soddy, Hart following. "I see you found it."

"Sure, we found it." Sammy Bean closed the door. "No trouble." He motioned toward the woman standing on the other side of the table. "John, this is Dolly Aims." He jerked his head at Hart. "And Ross Hart."

Both men took off their hats, Smith saying: "It's a pleasure, Miss Aims." Hart grunted something that sounded like "Howdy" and openly stared at the woman, with the naked lust of a sensual man.

"I'm happy to meet both of you," Dolly said. "How about a cup of coffee?"

"I'd like it," Smith said, and Hart grunted again and kept on staring.

"Sit down," Sammy said, motioning to a bench beside the table.

"Hell, no," Smith said. "I've had all the sitting I want for a while."

He watched Dolly walk to the stove and bring the coffee pot to the table and fill two tin cups and return to the stove, her buttocks flowing from side to side with the rhythm of her walk. Sammy was young, not over twenty, Smith knew, and he was surprised to find that Dolly was considerably older.

Smith sipped his coffee, wondering about that. He had known Sammy for more than two years and he did not have the slightest doubt about the boy's willingness and ability to carry out his part of this undertaking. He was not sure how many murders Sammy had committed, but he had heard of three.

Smith knew Ross Hart better than he did Sammy, their association going back for ten

112

years. Hart had a number of killings to his credit — at least five, not counting the Indians and Mexicans. His principal asset was his sharpshooting ability with a rifle, and it was that asset that had given Smith his reason for calling on Hart to take part in the operation. With Sammy, it had been a simple proposition of needing one more man who could be depended upon to carry out orders. This, he knew, was something Sammy Bean would do.

What about Dolly? She had turned to stand with her back to the stove, her hands folded in front of her, a forced smile on her full lips. She was not particularly pretty, but she wasn't ugly, either. She was big. Not fat or out of proportion, but she was taller than Sammy, and big-boned. Her pink blouse was pulled tightly across her breasts.

More than once Sammy had told Smith that Dolly was the best bed pardner he'd ever had and he aimed to hold onto her. From her point of view she probably had reason to want to hang onto Sammy. He had done very well the last year or so and Dolly loved money.

"By God," Sammy burst out, glaring at Hart, "you'd better get that idea out of your head. Dolly belongs to me and not to nobody else."

Hart looked at Smith. "What the hell's the matter with him? I haven't said anything."

"You don't need to," Sammy said. "I can read you every time you look at a woman."

Hart pretended that his feelings were hurt. He was a big man, six feet three inches and better than 200 pounds with long muscles and long bones and the easy grace of a man who has spent most of his life in the saddle. He had been in Arizona for the last three years except for short visits to Denver. The desert sun had burned his face a deep bronze so that anyone who didn't know him would have taken him for part Indian.

"I apologize if I looked at you wrong, Miss Aims," Hart said, his tone indicating he didn't mean a word of it.

"That's enough," Smith said. "You're so jealous you're a little crazy, Sammy. Now, how about it? Dolly's going to have the Dugan boy out here for twelve hours. Can you trust her?"

"I can trust her, all right," Sammy said. "I'm all the man she needs. It's this damned stud horse I don't trust."

"He won't see her again," Smith said. "Now, forget it." His gaze returned to the woman. "Dolly, this is a very delicate operation. It's been planned as exactly as it can be. A lot depends on you. I never saw you before, but I have heard about you."

"I'm flattered, Mister Smith," she said, making no attempt now to smile. "If you have heard that much of me, you know I'll do exactly what I say I will."

"Yes," Smith agreed. "That is one of two reasons I let Sammy bring you into this deal. The other reason is that I thought you were in love with Sammy. If anything goes wrong, I guess you know he'll get strung up with me and Ross."

"Both of your reasons are good ones," she said gravely. "I can promise you that nothing will go wrong out here."

"Good." Smith put his empty cup on the table and turned to Sammy. "What time did you get here?"

"After dark," Sammy said. "You gave us good directions. We rode along the ridge north of here and spotted the soddy before sundown. As soon as it was dark, we moved in."

Smith fished a cigar out of his coat pocket. He had been here before, so he knew where he and Hart were headed, but Sammy had never seen the place and Smith had been concerned that someone would notice Sammy and the woman ride in. He bit off the end of the cigar, struck a match, and lighted it, then he said: "All right, Dolly, what are you going to do?"

"Stay inside this stinking dirt house till noon tomorrow," she said. "We brought enough sandwiches and water so I won't have to go outside for anything. Sammy will fetch the boy here after a while and I'll see to it that he stays inside the soddy as long as I'm here." She turned to a shelf behind the stove and picked up a small revolver. "I'll kill him if I have to, but I don't think I will. I'm stout enough to handle any fourteen-year-old kid I ever saw."

"Fine," Smith said. "And after you leave here?"

"I'll tie him up before I leave so it'll take him a while to get loose," she said. "I'll saddle up and head back to the soddy where we stayed last night. I'll wait there for Sammy."

Smith nodded. "All right. Now, remember that our job is to kill the governor, which we will do exactly at noon tomorrow if everything goes on schedule. And it will, because the Amity bunch has a big program, and they'll have to run it tight if they're going to get everything in. Besides, the governor has to get back to Burlington in time to catch the eight o'clock train, so he's not going to be late showing up in Amity."

116

"I've heard there's a lot of people in Colorado who would like to shoot the governor," Hart said. "Maybe the Amity sheriff will be looking for something like this."

"Looking for it and stopping it are two different things," Smith said. "As long as we've got the boy out here, we can be clean gone before Dugan or the sheriff make a move. Whatever happens, Dugan won't sacrifice the life of his kid just to chase us."

"What about the bank money?" Sammy asked. "The last time we went over this, you hadn't made up your mind about it."

"Robbing the bank is the excuse we'll give for moving in on the Dugans," Smith answered. "If it works out so that Dugan gets back to his house with the money at noon, we'll take it. I see no reason to throw ten thousand dollars away if it drops into our hands. If it works out so Ross gets a chance to rub the governor out before noon, we'll get the job done and light out. Once we're in the sandhills, they'll never find us. We've got a relay of horses, so we won't be held up between here and Kansas. You have fresh horses at that soddy where you and Dolly stayed. By night we'll all be a long ways from here."

Sammy scratched his nose. "I hate to

overlook ten thousand dollars," he grumbled. "Seems to me we could work the timing so we'll get it for sure."

"It's not important," Smith said harshly. "We are hired for something else. That ten thousand is a plum that might fall into our laps. If so, good. If not, we forget it. The surest way to get ourselves hung is to be too greedy."

"All right, all right," Sammy said. "You're the boss."

"And you'd better remember it," Smith said. "Now then, we know the layout of the Dugan house. Ross and I will go in through the back door. Sammy, you will stay in the barn long enough to take the saddle off my horse. Ross's, too, but not yours. Then you come in, but stay in the kitchen unless I call you. From here on we play it by ear. Dugan has a meeting that will keep him from getting home early, but we don't know whether we'll beat him into the house or not. If we don't, we may need you for a reserve."

"I savvy," Sammy said.

"One other thing," Smith said. "We don't know where the girl, Jean, will be. The boy, Bud, will be in bed asleep, or should be unless something has gone wrong, but Jean's eighteen and engaged to the sheriff. They may be out buggy riding or something."

Hart snickered. "Yeah, something."

"Ross, Sammy's right about you," Smith said angrily. "You're a damn' stud horse. Now get this through your head. For the next twelve hours you're going to forget about women. We don't want a local crime to make these pumpkin rollers get any meaner than they will be after the governor's shot. You'll make enough out of this to hire all the women you want afterward."

"Sure," Ross said, "but don't expect me to forget about women for twelve hours. I can't do it that long."

"You'd better try damn' hard," Smith said.

"Who's hiring us?" the woman asked.

"That's something you'll never know," Smith said. "Neither does Sammy nor Ross. I don't know all of them myself. Well, it's time we got started. Sammy, saddle up. Ross, you go outside and look at the stars or something. I want a minute with Dolly."

Sammy hesitated, apparently not sure he could trust Smith with the woman, then he wheeled and left the soddy. Hart grinned and winked at Smith. "The kid's got it bad."

"So have I," Dolly said. "You'd better be damn' sure you don't let anything go wrong on your end."

"It's not our end I'm worried about," Smith said. "It's yours. As long as the boy is out here, we're in good shape. If you let him slip away and get into town, we're in trouble. It's that simple."

"I won't," she said sharply. "I keep telling you that, but you don't believe me."

Hart was gone now. Smith shut the door and turned to the woman. He said: "Dolly, I don't believe you because I know you might get scared being here by yourself with the boy. Well, I'll give you something to chew on that had better scare you. I know enough to hang you. If you bungle this and they catch me, I'll talk."

"Oh, hell." Dolly threw up her hands. "I'm not going to bungle it. Anyhow, I think you're lying."

Smith shook his head. "There isn't much that goes on in Denver I don't know. Now you want me to tell you what I know?"

"I sure do," she snapped. "I think you're bluffing with a pair of deuces."

"No, I'm holding a full house," he said. "There was a man named Pete Moss who got into bed with you one night a few months ago. They found him in an alley the next morning. Somebody shoved a butcher knife into his guts and took his money belt. You did it."

She stared at him, breathing hard, her breasts rising and falling like two great cushions, then she burst out: "You god-damned bastard!" She swallowed, and said: "I'll be double sure I don't bungle. I hope you do the same."

Smith turned and left the soddy, pulling the door shut behind him. Sammy and Hart were in their saddles, waiting. Smith mounted, and the three of them rode downslope toward the lights of Amity.

IV

Matt Dugan wiped his face with a hand as he glanced at the clock on the opposite wall. It was not quite midnight. He was impatient and he sensed that the others were impatient. They had waited about as long as they could for Uncle Pete Fisher and Jerry Corrigan; they were all tired and sleepy, and tomorrow was the big day.

Matt's office, in the rear of the bank, was hot, even though the windows and the back door were open. The evening had cooled off, but the little room still held the heat of the day. Matt felt the sweat roll down his face again. He couldn't stand sitting here any longer, and he started to say that they'd go ahead and get the meeting over with regardless of Fisher and Corrigan, when the front door opened.

He heard a man's heavy-footed walk and guessed it would be Uncle Pete Fisher. A moment later he saw he was right. The old man stopped in the doorway, his gaze touching Matt's face first, then turned to Jim Long, and finally to Cole Talbot and his wife Hannah. He had been drinking, Matt thought, or maybe he was just mad. He was mad most of the time these days, and Matt had wished more than once he had not appointed him a committee chairman of any kind.

"We almost gave you up," Matt said.

"I got delayed," Fisher said.

"Sit down, Pete." Matt motioned to a chair. "We'll wind this up fast. We need sleep right now more than we need planning. I'm tired."

"So am I." Fisher sat down, the chair groaning under his weight. "Sometimes I feel as old as my wife says I am."

They laughed, even Cole Talbot who was a dour and silent man. His wife Hannah's laugh was a high-pitched giggle that made Matt think she was always trying to make up for Cole's lack of laughter. Only Jim Long's laugh seemed natural. Matt knew his own was forced. He wished he could relieve his tensions by having a good case of hysterics the way his wife Nora did on occasion. Or maybe he ought to go out in the back yard and kick the dog.

"We'll make one quick run-down and go home," Matt said. "Did you see Jerry?"

Yeah, I saw him," Fisher said. "He ain't coming. He told me to tell you he was taking Jean buggy riding."

He said it with a kind of controlled fury that made Matt wonder if anything had happened, but he could not read the old man's expression, so he said: "It's all right. Jerry isn't a chairman of any committee. I just asked him to be here so he'd know what was going on." He picked up a sheet of paper from his desk and glanced at it. "Jim, all you have to do is to decorate the platform."

Jim Long nodded. He owned the Mercantile, Amity's biggest store. He was thirty-five, he had a wife and six children, and was baldheaded except for a fringe of hair around his head that looked like a black band. He had enough worries to lose his hair, Matt knew.

The panic of the previous year had been harder on Long than anyone else in Amity because he had carried too many people on his books and had borrowed from the bank more than Matt should have loaned him. If new people who were buying the irrigated land didn't have money to pay for what they bought in the Mercantile, Long would be the first to go down the drain.

"I had a talk with Pete," Long said, "and we decided to keep the band on the ground. That way we won't have to enlarge the platform. Putting up the bunting is the only thing left to do. We'll have it finished by ten o'clock."

"Good." Matt glanced at the paper. "Hannah, you have your crew picked and instructed, so I guess there's nothing more you can do tonight. I apologize for asking you to come tonight. . . ."

"I wanted to come," Hannah said, "because I've got something to say. I want all of you to hear it. Everything will be fine if the ladies get to the Methodist church by eight o'clock. What I want you to know is that, if they ain't there, we won't have the sandwiches made by one o'clock."

"We'll send the sheriff after them if they don't show up," Matt said.

Hannah sniffed. With one exception she was disdainful of everyone in town including her husband. The exception was Nora Dugan, the only person in Amity she honestly admired. She was thirty-five years old, childless, and difficult to get along with, a fact her husband knew better than anyone else.

Matt had not wanted to appoint Hannah chairman of the food committee, but he had been pushed into it because Cole, who ran the hotel, could handle the coffee making and bake the beans and furnish cups, plates, and silverware easier than anyone else. He was the one businessman in town who stood to make an immediate profit from the celebration. For the first time in years his hotel was full.

"I doubt that the sheriff will be on hand," Hannah said. "He'll be out somewhere sparking your Jean."

"I'll speak to him and Jean," Matt said. "Cole, I'll send Bud over first thing in the morning to help you set up the tables. You said you had the beans soaking, didn't you?"

"They're soaking," Talbot said in his sour way. "I'll get up at four and start the fire. I'll make enough coffee to take a bath in. Now I'm going to bed. I've wasted too much time already waiting for Pete to get here."

"One more thing," Matt said quickly, seeing the flare of anger in Pete Fisher's eyes. "The band assembles at eleven and they'll start playing at half past eleven. Right, Pete?" Fisher nodded, still staring trucu-

125

lently at Talbot. "Dick Miles has been told to get the governor here right at twelve. The minute you see Dick's rig, you get up on the platform and start the band playing that march we were talking about."

Fisher nodded again, turning his gaze to Matt. "If any of the band members ain't on hand at eleven, I will send the sheriff after 'em. Likewise I'll send him after Parson Hess if he figures on giving the invocation."

"Meeting adjourned," Matt said. "Thanks for coming. You can go to bed now, Cole."

Talbot muttered something about the meeting not being necessary in the first place. Hannah sniffed and Pete Fisher grumbled. The four left Matt's office, Jim Long the only one to say "Good night."

Matt remained at his desk for a time, thinking he was too tired to walk home. Besides, he was afraid to face Nora who had told him to be home by ten, that he was going to have a nervous breakdown if he didn't get some rest.

Nora was right. In fact, she was nearly always right. But there had been so many little things to settle, like where Jim Long would place the flag and which preacher would give the invocation and which one the benediction. It seemed to Matt that Hannah Talbot had been full of argument on every proposition that came up whether it was in her department or not.

Matt wiped his face and told himself that he had never been as tired as he was this minute. It was a strange, tense tiredness, not at all like the healthy fatigue he used to have when he'd been in the saddle for eighteen or twenty hours every day working roundup.

No, this was different, a kind of frantic nervousness that made it difficult to get agreement on even the simplest question. He understood why this was. Amity was trying to get up off the floor after being almost knocked out by the panic. With Matt leading, the businessmen of town, along with some of the ranchers, had borrowed enough money to finish the project. No one, not even Matt, could guarantee it would save the town, but he was positive of one thing. It would be complete disaster if it failed.

He rose and closed the back door and windows, then blew out the lamp, knowing he had to go home and get what rest he could. He left the office, blew out the bracket lamp near the front door, and, stepping outside, closed and locked the door.

"Matt," a man said.

He wheeled, startled, then saw Uncle Pete

127

Fisher standing a few feet from him, one of his cheap cigars clamped between his teeth. The moon was almost full, lighting Main Street with its yellow glow. None of the business places showed any light except the lobby of the Amity Hotel. The raucous noise that had flowed along Main Street earlier in the evening had died out until now the town actually seemed deserted.

"*Aw,* Pete," Matt said wearily. "I thought you'd be in bed by now."

"I want to talk a minute," Fisher said. "I'm a tired, bitter old man who had money most of his life and now don't have a dime. I live off what my wife inherited and wouldn't give me when it could have saved the bank, so I've got reason to be bitter. Even those damn' cigars I smoke would kill a horse. I dunno why they ain't killed me."

Matt knew all this except that Fisher was bitter. He had been angry ever since Matt invited Governor Wyatt to speak at the Dam Day celebration, but aside from that he had managed to hide his bitterness. He never refused to do anything he was asked, even to entertaining a bunch of kids with his tales about crossing the plains to California in 1849, or fighting in the Civil War, or battling Indians when he'd first settled out here on the plains and Amity had been nothing more than a store and a couple of sod houses.

"I never figured you for a bitter man, Pete," Matt said.

"Well, I am," Fisher said. "I know what it is to wind up your life a failure and not have it your fault. The man who's to blame is your god-damned Benjamin Wyatt. You and Jim and some of the others invited him before I knew anything about it. Now he's going to be here if you don't stop him, and he'll get himself shot. What will that do to Amity and all of our fine plans for auctioning off the land tomorrow?"

"Shot?" Matt couldn't get a breath for a moment, and, when he did, he asked hoarsely: "Pete, what the ding-dong hell ever gave you an idea like that?"

"It's all around if you wasn't deaf, dumb, and blind," Fisher said. "Your sheriff is in the same boat. I was talking to the Owl Creek boys in the Palace about Wyatt when Corrigan tried to make me shut up, then he tried to pull me out of the saloon and Yarnell jumped him. Corrigan clipped him on the chin and knocked him cold. He pulled a gun on Mason and Lupton and threw all three of 'em into the jug."

"Maybe if you'd kept your mouth

shut . . . ," Matt began.

"Why should I?" Fisher demanded. "Wyatt broke me, him and his Populist friends. But what I'm trying to tell you is that the Owl Creekers drove a jag of steers to Burlington and sold 'em for a song. They know Wyatt's responsible. They're the kind who'll rub him out tomorrow. The thing for you to do is to keep him out of town."

"I can't do that, Pete," Matt said. "By this time he's in Burlington. What's more, a lot of people who are in town came to hear the governor. Not because he's a Populist but because he's the governor. They'd be sore if he didn't show up."

"All right," Fisher said in a tight voice. "I guess you're running this show, but don't forget I warned you."

"Go home and go to bed," Matt said, and walked away.

He was so tired that he felt like laughing. Maybe he'd wind up having hysterics the way Nora did. You work and you scheme and you plan every little detail, you gamble your last dollar on your idea and you have every hope it will work, and then an old man who went broke trying to run a bank in your town starts talking about the governor's being murdered.

Ridiculous, he told himself, just plain

ridiculous. Still, he wished Pete Fisher had kept his mouth shut.

V

Nora Dugan put her sewing down when she heard the wall clock strike midnight. She was irritated, and she was going to let Matt know it when he came home. After a couple had been married twenty years, a man should know something about a wife's feelings, but it was evident Matt didn't know much about hers. If he did, he'd have come home an hour or more ago.

The truth was she was scared. Matt would laugh if she told him. He'd say that nothing bad ever happened in Amity, but tonight was different. A crowd of strangers was in town for the doings tomorrow, the governor coming and all. Earlier in the evening she had heard a lot of yelling and some shooting from Main Street that was less than two blocks away. You were bound to have a few toughs among so many strangers. Matt ought to know that.

She rose and walked to the front door and stood there, staring across the street at the park that was hidden from her sight by the darkness. She could lock both doors, but the heat was stifling even at midnight. The last few days had been inordinately hot for the Colorado plains, and, worse yet, the nights weren't cooling off. No, she had to leave both the front and back doors open to catch whatever breeze there was.

Of course she could latch the screens, but that wouldn't do any good if a man was determined to get into the house. It was easy enough to cut a hole in the wire netting and lift the latch. Bud was upstairs asleep, but he was only fourteen. Besides, he slept too soundly to be of any help if she needed it.

Maybe she was more worried about Jean than she thought. Funny thing, she reflected. You have children and you raise them to be independent and to look out for themselves. You try to prepare them to leave the family nest and build their own, but, when the time comes, you aren't ready for it and you think you can't give them up, not even your eighteen-year-old daughter who will be marrying the sheriff in a month.

Nora liked Jerry Corrigan. If she'd had her pick of all the eligible young bachelors in Amity or up and down Buffalo Creek, she would have chosen Jerry, red hair, freckles, and all. One thing was sure. He would take care of Jean. To Nora — and she guessed to all mothers — this was important.

Jerry wasn't what she considered handsome, but he was intelligent, strong, healthy; he was all she could ask for in a son-in-law, but the trouble was Jerry and Jean were so much in love they simply didn't have very good judgment right now.

Nora sighed and wished the month was up and they were getting married tomorrow. But they had set their date, so the only sensible wish for her to make at this moment was for Jerry to bring Jean home. He had not come for her until it was late and they hadn't been gone very long, but she wished Jean was home in bed. She was still just a girl.

Nora smiled, thinking this was silly. She wouldn't be like some women who kept on calling their daughters love names like "Doll" and "Baby" after they were grown and married and had their own children. Jean was eighteen. Nora had been only sixteen when she was married and Matt had been nineteen. Actually they were still young. She was thirty-five and Matt was thirty-eight.

If this dam project failed and he lost the bank, they could go back to ranching. In some ways she thought they would be better off ranching than living in town with Matt worrying about hard times and the interest people weren't paying on their mortgages and Uncle Pete Fisher who kept trying to tell Matt how to run the bank.

She stiffened. She heard a sound back of the house. She wasn't sure what it was, but she thought it was the shed door being closed. Matt had probably come down the alley and was checking the horses. He kept two in town, Big Red, a sorrel saddle horse, and Dolly, the mare he used for driving.

There were times when Nora thought she had a right to be jealous. Matt was a little insane when it came to horses. She smiled as she thought about it. You could take a rancher off the ranch and put him in a bank, but you didn't take the ranch out of the rancher. Matt Dugan was still a cowman at heart, and she guessed that was the way she wanted it.

She heard the back screen open and turned toward the kitchen. It was all fine and dandy for Matt to get involved in the big celebration tomorrow. In fact, she was involved, too, because she had promised to help Mrs. Talbot with the sandwiches in the morning, but Matt had gone too far.

He was the general chairman, the hub of the wheel. This whole thing would never have gotten off the ground if he hadn't spent hour after hour attending meetings, if he hadn't threatened and begged and twisted arms. But to be this late on the last night. . . .

She stopped, her mouth open, her heart jumping into her throat. Two strange men were coming toward her. She leaned against the wall, her knees threatening to buckle under her. Now that it was too late, she told herself, she had known something like this would happen, but she had insisted on ignoring the warning.

"You're Missus Dugan?" the man in front asked.

She tried to speak, to tell them to get out of the house, but her lips could not form the words. The man who had spoken was about forty, she judged, small and dark with eyes as bright as a chipmunk's. Apparently he was a city man, well dressed in a brown broadcloth suit, a white shirt, and a black string tie. He carried a revolver in a holster on his right hip. It seemed to her that the gun was not in keeping with his manner or his clothes.

The other man was a cowboy. At least he wore range clothes. He carried a rifle in his right hand and had a revolver in a holster that was exactly in keeping with his manner and clothes. He was big, taller and broader of shoulder even than Matt. He was rough-featured, with a week-old stubble on his face, and was younger than the small one, probably in his late twenties.

She didn't know much about things like this, but Matt had served one term as sheriff several years ago, and she remembered his saying that a professional gunman carried his pistol low on his hip and tied it to his thigh. That was the way the big man carried his.

The two men were silent, waiting for Nora to answer the question, but all she could do was to nod. The small man said: "Believe me, Missus Dugan, we have no wish to harm you. All we ask is that you obey orders. Is your husband home?"

Again she tried to speak, but she still could not make a word come out of her mouth. She had always been a strong, self-reliant woman. A ranch wife had to be and she had prided herself on being a good one, but now her insides were jelly. She shook her head and was ashamed that fear had so completely possessed her.

"All right, we'll talk to him when he gets here," the man said. "Let's go into your front room and sit down. Remember that we will not hurt you or any of your family if you co-operate. You are an attractive woman and I understand that your daughter is equally attractive, but let me repeat what I said. We will not touch either of you unless you force us to."

She walked into the front room and sat down in her rocking chair, her legs feeling as if they were stilts. Both of her legs and arms were cold, even though her face was damp with perspiration. The small man dropped into the black leather couch that was across the room from Nora, but the big one stood a few feet away, his gaze fixed on her.

"I'm John Smith," the small man said, smiling slightly. "You've never heard of me, but you have heard of my friend." He nodded at the big man. "His name is Ross Hart." He stopped, apparently expecting her to be impressed, or frightened. The name did sound vaguely familiar, but she could not pin an identity to it.

"You and your husband sleep downstairs," Smith said. "Upstairs you have two bedrooms and a sewing room which is next to the street and looks out on the park that surrounds the courthouse. One of these bedrooms is occupied by your daughter Jean, the other by your son Bud. Am I right?"

She was breathing easier, her heart had dropped back to its normal position, and she had begun to believe he meant it when he'd said that they did not intend to hurt her or her family. Now her curiosity began to work, and she asked: "How do you know so much about us?"

She did not recognize her own voice, but at least she was able to speak. She felt a prickle slide down her spine. She glanced at Hart and saw that his pale blue eyes were pinned on her. She looked away, but still she felt his gaze. She sensed something unspeakably evil about the man as if he were an animal who was disguised as a man.

"Never mind how we know." Smith laughed softly. "You will find that we know a great deal about you and your family, Missus Dugan. Now then, where is Bud?"

"In bed asleep."

"Jean?"

"She's out buggy riding with the sheriff." Nora clenched her fists and leaned forward. "He'll bring her home any minute. If you know what's good for you, you will both get out of here before he does."

"Now why should we do that?" Smith asked.

"Because if you're still here when he comes in, I'll have him arrest you."

"No, I wouldn't advise that, Missus Dugan," Smith said. "That sort of talk will get you hurt. If he does come into the house, you will introduce us as your cousins from the western slope who unexpectedly dropped in on you. You don't have room for us, but you'll put us up some way because every room in town is taken. Is that right?"

"Yes, but he won't believe that."

"It's up to you to lie so well that he does believe you. I want to be honest with you and Mister Dugan when he gets here. You have a choice. You can co-operate and you will not be hurt, or you can get your family killed. It's that simple. Your sheriff may be hell on high, red wheels, but he can't handle both of us."

She wiped her face with her handkerchief. It wasn't just the heat that was making her perspire. It was fear. Her heart was in her throat again. She believed this man Smith. He was soft-spoken and courteous, but it was only a veneer. She felt a ruthlessness about him that was almost as terrifying as the animal-like evil she had sensed in Ross Hart.

"Good," Smith said when she nodded. "You have made the right choice. I hope you will stay with it. One more thing. When will your husband be home?"

"I thought he'd be home before this," she said in a low tone.

"Then he should be along any time," Smith said. "Ross, take one of the lamps and go upstairs. See how her sewing room looks."

Hart picked up a lamp that was on the oak center table and climbed the stairs, his rifle still in his right hand. Nora hunched forward, her small hands tightly clenched. She wondered if she could lunge across the room and reach Smith before he could draw his gun. She had not really made her choice.

She did not know what they intended to do, but death might be far better than what would happen if these men had their way with her. When she remembered the expression on Hart's face, she knew she would prefer death, but then she thought of Matt and Jean and Bud, and she realized the choice was not hers to make.

VI

Matt angled across a corner of the park on his way home, pausing for a moment beside the platform from which the governor would speak tomorrow. He tried, but he could not free his mind of what Uncle Pete Fisher had said.

Suppose the governor was shot while he was here? It would give Amity a black eye whether the people of Amity had anything to do with it or not. What was worse, it would probably arouse public sentiment to such a wild fury that it would kill the dam project.

He went on toward his house, telling himself that at least he would talk to Jerry Corrigan. They could watch out for an assassin. Maybe they could stop him in time, and he knew at once this was foolish thinking. The murder would be committed, the crowd would be thrown into an uproar with no one being sure what had happened, and in the chaos that was bound to follow the killer would probably get away.

Matt crossed the street to the gate in the picket fence in front of his house, gloomily making note of the fact that the lamps in the front room were still lighted. He sighed, telling himself he had known all the time that Nora would stay up until he came home, even though she needed the sleep as much as he did.

As usual the gate *squealed* when it was opened. The sound irritated him. He had told Bud a dozen times to oil the hinges, but the boy could think of a number of things he'd rather do, with the result that the gate still squealed. Maybe it was a good idea to keep the gate that way. It warned people who were in the house that someone was coming.

One thing was sure. Jean couldn't slip in at two o'clock in the morning and then blandly brag about being so quiet that no one heard her come in at only half past twelve. It wasn't really important. Jean would be married and gone in a month. Nora worried about the girl, but that was a natural fault of any mother.

Matt smiled as he walked up the path to his front door. He had a mental picture of Jean: a tow-headed girl who loved to ride and romp with Bud and could still hold her own with him in a tussle. He found it hard to accept the fact that she had become a young lady old enough and mature enough to marry Jerry Corrigan. Matt would be thirty-nine in another year, a year that would probably make him a grandfather. He grimaced at the thought.

He opened the front screen and stepped inside, pausing to hang his hat on the hall tree. Nora told him he ought to start wearing a derby, that it was more fitting for a banker than the sweat-stained old Stetson that had been bucked off his head and been down in the manure of a corral more than once. It was a carry-over from his ranching days, and like his worn boots it was so comfortable that he couldn't bring himself to throw it away.

Matt went into the front room, knowing that Nora would be sitting there waiting for him. She would be angry, but he'd get around her some way. He opened his mouth to apologize to her, but the apology was never made.

The instant Matt appeared in the doorway, Nora lunged out of her chair and charged across the room at a strange man who was sitting on the couch, her hands in front of her as if she had every intention of clawing his eyes out.

Matt had no idea who the man was or why he was here, or even what Nora was trying to do. He took one more step, moving automatically, and stopped as the man rose and slapped Nora on the side of the face, a hard blow that rocked her head and sent her reeling halfway back toward her chair.

For an instant Matt was paralyzed, completely dumbfounded by the scene he had stumbled into, a scene he would never expect to see in his own front room. Then he recovered. He yelled an oath and dived at the man, filled with an insane desire to kill the stranger with his hands. He was still ten feet away when something crashed against his head sending him to his knees, Nora's scream ringing in his ears.

For a good part of a minute Matt stayed on his knees, blood dribbling down the side of his face. He wasn't unconscious, but he wasn't fully conscious, either. Nora's screams seemed to run on and on. He couldn't get up, and yet he somehow managed to keep from falling forward on his face. He wanted to smash the man who had struck Nora, but he couldn't move.

"I warned you not to do anything like that, Missus Dugan," the man said. "I told Sammy to stay in the kitchen out of sight just on the chance you might be foolish, and you were. I hope you have learned your lesson. If you haven't, some people you love will get killed."

"He's hurt," Nora said. "Help me get him to the couch so he can lie down."

"Give her a hand, Sammy," the man said. "If there is any more trouble, my gun is the one that will be used. My gun is for shooting, Missus Dugan. I do not club people on the head with it."

Matt heard the talk, but the words seemed to be floating to him from a great distance. His head felt as if someone were pounding on it in a steady rhythm.

They lifted him to his feet, Nora on one side, the man who had slugged him on the other. The room tipped and turned in front of him as he staggered the few feet to the couch. He lay down, the incessant beating on his head not stopping even for a moment.

"Let me get a wet cloth on his head," Nora said. "Please."

"You brought this on, Missus Dugan," the man said. "I told you, when I first came in, I had no desire to hurt you or your family. If you could really understand that, and make up your mind to co-operate, we'll get along a lot better."

"I understand it now," Nora said. "Will you please let me go to the kitchen and get a wet cloth?"

"Of course," the man said. "Go with her, Sammy. We can't trust her after what she just did. If she tries anything foolish again, shoot her."

This must be a nightmare, Matt thought. It couldn't be happening, not in Amity where a drunken brawl was the most disturbing thing that ever happened. Or in his own home where an argument between Jean and Bud about Bud's getting out of the parlor when Jean and Jerry wanted to sit there, or about who was going to help Nora with the dishes was the worst that he could imagine.

He sat up and fell back at once, the pain in his head so agonizing that he had to clench his teeth to keep from crying out. He heard a groan and felt foolish when he realized he was the one who had made the sound. If he only knew what was going on — if he had a gun — if Jean would get back and bring Jerry into the house. But it was all wishful thinking. The fact was they were in one hell of a tight fix.

Nora knelt beside the couch and wiped the blood from his face, then she laid the wet cloth across his forehead. "Honey," she whispered, "I'm so sorry. I didn't know there were three of them. One went upstairs and I thought there was just this one man down here. I tried to . . . oh, I should have done what he told me."

"That's right," the man said, standing behind her. "You forgot what I told you about Ross, that if you made trouble down here, he'd kill Bud. This was close, Missus Dugan. If Sammy hadn't nailed your husband the second he did, Bud would be dead and you would have nobody but yourself to blame."

"I told you I learned my lesson," Nora said.

She tried to choke back a sob, but she could not. She sat on the floor beside the couch, a handkerchief to her eyes. The man waited for a few seconds, staring at her as if not quite sure of her yet, then he said: "All right, Missus Dugan, we'll go on that basis."

He stood over Matt, scratching his nose, his forehead furrowed. After a moment's silence, he said: "Can you hear me and understand what I'm saying, Dugan? I know your head hurts like hell, but we've got some things to talk about. The sooner you get this deal straightened out in your mind, the better."

Matt heard, but his head was still pounding. Nora had not moved from where she sat on the floor. Apparently Bud was asleep upstairs. Matt figured Jean was still out with Jerry. When they got back, Jerry might come into the house with her. He usually did just for a minute. That could be the only chance they had to get these men off their backs.

A bluff might work, Matt thought. "You'd better clear out before the sheriff comes in with our daughter," he said.

The man laughed. "Your wife tried that, Dugan. Your head's too thick for you to figure things out, so I'll figure them out for you. Your boy, Bud, is asleep upstairs. Our friend, Ross Hart, is also upstairs. If you or

147

your wife or your sheriff upsets our little apple cart, the boy dies. I'm going upstairs to look around. Now you just lie there and think about what I said. Maybe your head will ache a hell of a lot worse after you get done thinking."

He left after telling Sammy to watch them. Matt closed his eyes. He heard the rumble of talk from upstairs, and even though he still wasn't able to keep his mind focused on what was happening or on what might be a way out of their trouble, one thing came clear. If he tipped off Jerry and Jerry jumped these men, Bud would die. That, of all things, must not happen.

VII

Matt lost all sense of time. He lay on the couch with the wet cloth over his eyes, the pounding in his head gradually becoming less violent. Nora had not moved from where she sat on the floor beside the couch.

He did not open his eyes until he heard the man say: "All right, Dugan. Are you able to listen to me?"

He looked at the man, rolling his head just a little on the cushion. Even that slight movement started the racketing in his head again. He guessed that the man had not

148

been upstairs more than five minutes, but he knew he had to listen, had to figure out some way to fool Jean and Jerry Corrigan when they came in.

"Go ahead," Matt said.

"Good," the man said. "My name is John Smith. The young man who hit you is Sammy Bean. You have never heard of us, but you have heard of Ross Hart, who is upstairs. He's a killer, Dugan. We all are, if necessary, but Sammy's young and I don't like killing. I hate to even kill an animal. Real chicken-hearted, you might say."

Matt stared past Smith at the young fellow who had hit him. He was hardly a man, although Matt could not guess his age. His beardless face was almost girlish. He was average height and thin, with fine features and a knife-lipped mouth that held a smirking grin.

"No use to lie to him," Sammy Bean said. "I'm as much of a killer as Ross. I ain't as old. That's all."

John Smith nodded. "That's right, Sammy. Give yourself a year or two and you'll have as many notches on your gun as Ross has. What I'm trying to tell you, Dugan, is a simple equation of time and space. I have said this before and I will say it again because it is of life and death importance to you. I don't want to hurt any of you. At the risk of boring you, I'm being repetitious. Is that clear?"

"It's clear," Matt said.

"Now, then. Ross Hart is upstairs. Your boy, Bud, is asleep upstairs. If the sheriff comes in with your daughter, and if you get the idea through to him that you're in trouble, he will draw his gun and he'll die. So will you, but regardless of what happens to you or the sheriff or your women, the boy will die the instant Ross hears a shot from down here. I should explain that I really don't give a damn whether your family lives or dies, but I am very anxious that our plan succeeds. That's why I don't want any shots fired. It's to our interest as well as yours that you co-operate all the way."

"We will," Matt said, "but if you've gone to all this trouble to rob us. . . ."

"Save your energy, Dugan," Smith said. "We did not go to all this trouble just to rob you. You won't like what we're going to do. That's why I have said repeatedly that your lives depend on your co-operation. If you fully understand that, I'm hopeful that you will co-operate even though you hate like hell to do it."

Matt reached down beside the couch and took Nora's hand. He still had no idea what kind of a devil's scheme Smith had planned, but he was convinced that these men were not bluffing. He was unable at the moment to identify the name Ross Hart, but he had read about the man in the newspaper. Sooner or later he would remember what he had read.

He glanced at Sammy Bean who stood behind Smith, grinning like an idiot. Matt couldn't tell whether he was average bright or short on brains, but one thing was sure — Sammy's brag about being as much of a killer as Ross Hart was true.

"We'll co-operate," Matt said.

"I think I just heard a buggy in the street," Smith said. "It might be your daughter and her sheriff friend. If I'm right, we don't have much time. How about you, Missus Dugan?"

"I've already said. . . ."

"I want to hear you say it again," Smith said.

"I'll co-operate," Nora said, her voice trembling.

"All right," Smith said. "When Jean and the sheriff come in, tell them that Sammy and I are your cousins from the western slope. We arrived unexpectedly this evening to take in the celebration tomorrow. Ross Hart works for us. We'll stay here tonight

151

and pull out tomorrow because we can't leave our business in Grand Junction any longer than that. We're cattle buyers. We'll buy a small herd and drive it down the Grand. I think your sheriff will accept that story."

"Jean won't," Matt said. "She knows we don't have any relatives on the other side of the mountains."

"Then you'd better be damned sure you convince her," Smith said, his voice turning brittle.

"We'll try," Matt said.

"We'll be here twelve hours," Smith said. "After that the prairie will swallow us. You'll never have a chance to track us. Just be satisfied if you're all alive by then."

Matt couldn't stand it any longer. He burst out: "What are you up to? You've been beating the devil around the bush threatening us until. . . ."

"I'm ready to tell you," Smith said. "We're bank robbers. We know that you borrowed ten thousand dollars and it came in on the stage a day or so ago. That's what we're after. Our scheme is more efficient and safer than walking in and holding you up. We know you have more *dinero* in your vault, but we're hoping you'll be willing to cooperate if we don't clean you out."

Matt started to sit up and fell back at once. For a few seconds he thought his head would explode. He moistened his dry lips with the tip of his tongue. He said: "That ten thousand was borrowed to finish the dam. Do you know what stealing it will do to me and the town and the entire county? Do you have any idea how tough it is to raise ten thousand dollars in times as hard as these?"

"Yes, I do have some idea," Smith said. "That's why we're here. It's why we planned this scheme out to the last little detail."

"Just how do you think you'll get that *dinero* by moving in on us?" Matt asked.

"By you bringing it to us," Smith answered. "We'll stay here in your house until a few minutes after noon tomorrow. At that time everybody will be in the park listening to the governor. That's when you will bring the money to us. Nobody is going to pay any attention to you while you're doing it or to us while we're leaving town."

"Of all the stupid, crazy. . . ."

"Oh no," Smith said. "Not stupid and not crazy. You will put the money in a sack or satchel or whatever you have and bring it to us and we will get on our horses and ride like hell out of town. No one knows we're here. We came at midnight when no one saw us. We will leave at noon while the crowd is listening to the governor." He raised his hand when Matt started to say something. "Don't tell me what you won't do, Dugan. You don't want your son and daughter killed, so you will rob your own bank just as I'm telling you to do."

Outside the gate *squealed* as it was opened. Jean and Jerry were coming in.

He heard the front door open, he heard Jean laugh and say something to Jerry, and in that instant he breathed a prayer that God would help him lie so convincingly that Jean and Jerry would believe him.

VIII

When Jerry Corrigan left town with Jean, he drove directly to the ridge overlooking the dam site. There he pulled up and kissed Jean, and then put an arm around her and drew her to him. A moment later she went to sleep on his shoulder. He sat motionlessly, not wanting to disturb her; he thought about his future and wondered how any man could be as lucky as he was.

His ranch was downstream on the south side of the creek, 160 acres of land that would be irrigated when the project was finished. That would be soon, now that the money had been raised. The strange part of it was a few years ago no one had thought about building a dam on Buffalo Creek and nothing but sheer luck had caused him to select that particular quarter-section.

Not long ago his place was considered almost worthless. The only thing it had been good for was range, and you couldn't run many head of cattle on a quarter-section covered by sagebrush, Spanish bayonet, and a little buffalo grass.

Now, with the completion of the project assured, his homestead was worth a small fortune. He was not going to run for sheriff in the fall, and, as soon as his term was over, he and Jean would move onto his place. There was only a soddy there now, but he could borrow any reasonable amount from the bank to improve it. The fact that the president of the bank, Matt Dugan, was to be his father-in-law didn't make any difference. Only one thing was important. He owned a valuable piece of land.

Jean stirred in his arms. "It must be late, Jerry. We've got to go home."

"Why?" he demanded. "In a month you'll be Missus Jerry Corrigan. You're a grown woman. It's your business if you want to stay out all night with me."

Jean giggled. "Oh, yes, Mister Corrigan.

I'm a grown woman, so I can violate all the rules I want to."

"Well, can't you? If your ma and Matt don't trust you with me at your age. . . ."

"Jerry, be reasonable." She straightened and drew away from him. "Of course they trust me, and the day we're married we can come out here and sit up all night in a buggy if that's what you want to do. Personally I'd rather go to bed."

"Well, yes," he admitted, "so would I."

"Until then, I will live at home," she said, "and, as long as I live at home, I will have to put up with family rules."

He was silent for a moment. He had learned a great deal about family rules and family loyalty and family love in the months since Jean had promised to marry him. He never had had a family, at least not one he could remember. His parents had died when he was a baby, and an aunt and uncle had taken him to raise but not to love. The beatings and the man work he'd had to do had been too much, so he had run away when he was twelve and had made his own way since.

The Dugans had taken him in as if he really were their son. He could not ask for a better relationship with anyone than he had with Jean's parents. He got along fine with

Bud, too. Any way he looked at it, he'd be stupid to antagonize them.

"I guess you're right about family rules," he said, "but I hope your folks will let us make our own rules after we're married."

"They will, honey," she said. "I'm sure they will. Now will you take me home and deliver me to my parents?"

"Your slightest wish is a command to be obeyed," he said as he unwrapped the lines from the brake handle.

He spoke to the horse as he slipped an arm around her. They rode in silence for a time except for the steady *clip-clop* of hoofs in the dust of the road.

"Let's get married now," he said suddenly. "Tomorrow. We can drive to Burlington and get married first thing in the morning. I can't wait a whole month."

"You're just trying to get out of a church wedding," she said.

"That's part of it," he admitted.

"It won't do you a bit of good, Mister Corrigan," she said. "As much as I want to get married, we'll have to wait. It would kill Mama if we ran away to get married. We will have a church wedding, Parson Hess will marry us, and we will have a reception afterward. These coming events are unalterable, so make up your mind to live through them."

He sighed. "I guess I'm just a dreamer."

"You surely are," she murmured. "Besides, you can't go off and leave Amity without protection tomorrow."

He thought of the governor's coming and about what Uncle Pete Fisher had said and about the Owl Creek ranchers he had jailed, and he wished he could go fishing and forget the whole thing. Then he wondered why he even let such a thought enter his mind. He never had walked away from a dangerous situation and he wasn't starting now.

"No," he said, "I guess I can't."

They were in town then. Main Street was dark except for the lobby of the Amity Hotel. Corrigan turned left when he reached the park block and a moment later pulled up in front of Jean's home.

"Your folks must be sitting up for you, with all those lamps lighted," he said. "They usually just keep the hall lamp lighted for you, don't they?"

"Yes," she answered. "I don't know why they'd be sitting up for me tonight." She hesitated, then added: "Unless there's some kind of trouble."

"Maybe Matt's not back from the meeting yet," Corrigan said as he stepped down.

He walked around the rig and gave Jean a hand, then opened the gate that *squealed* as loudly as ever, and stood to one side while Jean went through. He held her hand as they walked up the path. When they reached the front door, he took her by the shoulders and turned her to face him.

"I got short-changed on the kissing to-night," he said. "You went to sleep on me."

"It was just that I had such a nice shoulder to sleep on," she said. "I'll make it up to you right now."

She did. A moment later he said: "Now I'll go to my room and see if I can get my breath back."

She opened the door and giggled as she patted his cheeks. "You do that, darling," she said. "Now come in and say good night to my folks if they're still up."

He followed her into the hall. She stopped when she reached the door into the front room. He heard Nora say: "We have a surprise, Jean. Your cousins, John and Sammy, got in a little while ago. They're here for the celebration tomorrow. You know, I don't think you ever met them."

Jerry stopped behind Jean. He was almost as surprised as she was because he had never heard her mention any cousins named John and Sammy. The one Nora had called

John rose and came to them, his hand extended.

"If I had known I had a cousin as attractive as you," he said, "I'd have been here a long time ago." He shook hands with Jean and turned to Jerry and offered his hand. "I didn't catch your name."

"I'm sorry," Nora said quickly. "Jerry Corrigan, our sheriff. Jerry, this is my sister's son, John Smith." She motioned to the second man. "Sammy Bean, meet Sheriff Corrigan."

Jerry shook hands with Smith, then Bean, and decided he didn't like either man. Maybe it was because they had moved in on the Dugans without warning on a day when they didn't have time to entertain guests.

"I had better explain how it is," Smith said to Jean, smiling. "You see, my mother was a sort of black sheep. She was much older than your mother and ran away from home with my father. He died, and she married Hank Bean, Sammy's father. My mother and Nora never had much to do with each other, but I took a chance on Nora being big-hearted and putting us up for the night." He turned to Corrigan. "I understand the hotel is full."

"That's right," Corrigan said.

Jean's face was pale. She glanced at Corrigan who stood beside her, then at her mother. "I never heard of any cousins with your names," she said, turning to Smith. "Or of your black sheep mother."

"I never talked about them," Nora said quickly. "It's like John said. We never had much to do with each other."

"As a matter of fact," Smith said, "we're here on business. Sammy and I hope to buy some cattle if we can get them for the right price. We'll be leaving after the celebration tomorrow. Next time we'll stay long enough to get acquainted, Jean. I'm ashamed that we waited so long to visit you."

Corrigan turned to Matt who was lying on the couch and hadn't said a word since the two of them had come in. He asked: "What's the matter with you, Matt?"

He grinned, or tried to. "I'm ashamed to admit it, Jerry, but I stumbled in front of the house. I fell down and must have hit my head on a rock."

"Knocked himself cold," Smith said. "It's a good thing we were here. I don't know how Nora could have got him into the house by herself."

"We lugged him in like a sack of wool," Sammy Bean said.

Corrigan glanced at Bean. He kept grinning as if he wasn't quite bright. He had a gun, but that was natural enough if the two men were cattle buyers as Smith had said.

Smith was the one that made Corrigan wonder about them. He had city written all over him. He had absolutely no family resemblance to Bean. He was older and smoother, a very courteous man who wore a brown broadcloth suit with a gold chain across his vest. From the way he kept fumbling with an elk tooth charm that dangled from the chain, Corrigan judged he was nervous and wondered why.

"I'd better get along," Corrigan said. "We'll have a lot of excitement tomorrow."

"I'm sure you will," Smith said. "It isn't every day that the governor comes to Amity."

"That's right," Nora said.

"Good night," Corrigan said, glancing at Jean and hoping she would go with him as far as the porch so he could kiss her again before he left.

But Jean apparently wasn't even thinking about another kiss. She stood with her back stiff, her eyes pinned on her mother. She said: "Mama, I'd like for Jerry to spend the night here."

"I'm sorry," Nora said. "You know we'd

love to have him any other time, but we don't have room for him tonight. You see, they brought a friend named Ross Hart with them. He's going to sleep on the cot in my sewing room."

Corrigan looked at Jean, wondering what put a crazy notion like that into her head. He wondered, too, if there was something about these cousins that scared her, then dismissed the thought as being one of those harebrained ideas that came to her occasionally. He guessed he was a little scared himself about what might happen tomorrow.

"No reason for me to sleep here, Jean," Jerry said. "I'm paying for a room, so I might as well use it."

He nodded at no one in particular and left the house, still wondering why Jean had wanted him to stay there all night when it was plain enough the house was already overcrowded. He stepped into the buggy and drove back to Main Street and left the rig and horse in the livery stable.

As he walked to the hotel, the name Ross Hart popped into his mind. Nora had mentioned it casually, a friend of Smith's and Bean's who was going to sleep in Nora's sewing room. "Ross Hart!" He said it aloud, telling himself that the name was familiar, but he couldn't pin anything to it.

He shrugged and climbed the stairs to his room. He'd think about it tomorrow. Tonight he was too tired to think about anything.

IX

No one made a move for several minutes after Jerry Corrigan left the house. Matt lay on the couch, listening for the buggy to wheel on down the street. Nora and Jean remained where they had been when Corrigan left, their heads cocked as if they, too, were listening. Sammy Bean stood a few feet from Jean, his right hand on the butt of his gun, his gaze on the girl. John Smith, standing near the foot of the stairs, was the most relaxed person in the room.

"He's gone," Smith said after the silence had run on until it had become unbearable to Matt. "You were stupid, young lady." He nodded at Jean. "Next time you had better find out what the situation is before you ask the sheriff to stay overnight."

Jean turned to stare at Smith. "It's time somebody told me what the situation is," she snapped. "Who are you and why are you here?"

"I'm John Smith," he said. "We have come

to rob the bank, with your father's assistance, of course."

"That's a bad joke," she said. "I want to know why you're here and telling this crazy lie about being my cousins."

"It's no joke," Smith said, nodding at Matt. "Ask your father."

"I'm afraid they have a plan to rob the bank, all right," Matt said. "They think I'll bring ten thousand dollars home at noon tomorrow and they'll ride out of the town with the money while everybody's excited about the governor getting here."

Jean's face had turned pale. "I don't believe this is real. I must be having a nightmare."

"It's not a nightmare," Smith said, "though if any of you, including your sheriff friend, fail to co-operate, it will turn out to be a hell of a nightmare. Believe me." He motioned at Matt. "Stand up. I want to see if you can. Sammy may have slugged you harder than I intended. You've got to be feeling good tomorrow."

Matt rose from the couch. Again he thought his head would explode, but he stood motionlessly for a few seconds as the floor pitched and rolled in front of him. Gradually the hammering inside his skull faded to a dull headache as the floor leveled out so that it appeared normal.

"Are you all right?" Nora asked anxiously.

"Sure, I'm fine," Matt answered.

"Good." Smith nodded at Nora. "Missus Dugan, you and Jean might as well sit down. You won't be going to bed for a while." He turned to Matt. "Dugan, where are your guns?"

Matt motioned toward the hall door. "Yonder in a room we call my office. Bring a lamp," Matt suggested, and walked toward the hall door.

He moved slowly because he was still dizzy. He stopped and clenched his fists as the floor started to whirl in front of him again. When it stopped, he went on. Smith picked up a lamp from the center table and caught up with him, calling back to Nora: "Missus Dugan, you explain to Jean why it will be a nightmare if she doesn't co-operate!"

Smith followed Matt across the hall into the room on the other side. It was furnished with a desk, a swivel chair, a small table, and two rawhide-bottom chairs. A small safe was in one corner. Three deer heads were on the wall. A shotgun and two rifles were racked on the antlers. A Colt .45 in a holster attached to a cartridge belt hung from a nail near the door.

Smith took the shotgun and rifles down from the antler racks and pulled the revolver from the holster. He asked: "These the only guns in the house?"

"That's right," Matt answered.

"If you're lying and I find a hide-out gun . . . ," Smith began.

"Let me tell you something once and for all." Matt leaned against the wall, his knees threatening to turn to rubber. "I served a term as sheriff and I've ridden with a dozen posses. I've taken several men to the state pen, and I can honestly say I never met a man I wanted to kill as much as I do you. If I get a chance, I'll do it with my bare hands, but not until I can do it without putting my family in danger. As long as they are in danger, I'll do exactly what you tell me."

"Good," Smith said. "I'm not concerned what you think of me or the safety of your family, but I am concerned about the success of our plan. We have worked on it too long to fail, now that we're this close to succeeding." He gestured toward the front room. "Wake Bud up and have him dress. Then bring him downstairs."

"How do you come to know so much about us?" Matt asked.

"Let's say I've been informed," Smith said. "It was part of the plan. We'll let it go at that. I think you and your family will be safer if you don't know any more."

They returned to the front room, Smith setting the lamp down on the table and the guns in a corner. Matt crossed to the stairs and started to climb them, not stopping until Nora cried: "What are you going to do?"

"Smith told me to wake Bud and have him dress," Matt said, pausing on the third step and looking back at Nora.

She whirled to face Smith. "Why?" she demanded. "Do you have to bring a boy into this . . . this terrible scheme of yours?"

"Yes, I have to," Smith said. "You will all be safer because I am bringing a boy into it. You might call him a hostage. He's our guarantee you will co-operate. I admire your courage, Missus Dugan, but not your judgment. As long as the boy is our hostage, you will co-operate. Otherwise, you might be tempted to do something that would bring disaster to all of you."

Nora's hands were fisted at her sides; her face was white and drawn, and her temples were throbbing as if the blood was threatening to break out. Matt, knowing the violence of her temper, was afraid she would do something foolish now.

"Nora," Matt said sharply, and came back

down the stairs and crossed the room to her. "Listen to me." He took her hands and found they were as cold as if she had just soaked them in ice water. "I've told Smith I'd kill him if I had a chance to do it without putting my family in danger, but until I get that chance, I'll do exactly what he tells me. I want you to do the same."

Nora swallowed, staring at Smith with a venomous hatred. She nodded slowly. "All right, Matt," she whispered.

Jean had dropped into a chair. She rose and, coming to her mother, put an arm around her. "Let's sit down on the couch," Jean said. "Let's try to do what Dad says."

Nora let herself be led to the couch. Matt waited till they sat down. When he was sure that Nora had regained control of herself, he turned and climbed the stairs. He found a man sitting at their head, a Winchester across his knees. Matt stopped, surprised that he was there.

In spite of all the talk about Ross Hart, Matt had not fully grasped the fact that the man was actually in the house, or that he had been watching the scene below him in the front room. Now for the first time Matt understood why Smith had been so sure of himself. If Jerry Corrigan had caught on to what was happening and had drawn his gun,

Hart would have cut him down at once.

A bracket lamp was burning about ten feet down the hall. When Matt stopped, Hart turned his head and grinned, a wicked grin that mocked Matt. His face was dark, but his eyes were pale blue. They might have been made of glass, there was so little expression in them.

"He gave you the notion I'm a son-of-a-bitch, didn't he?" Hart asked.

"He's given me the notion you all are," Matt said.

"Oh, John ain't," Hart said. "He's real polite and he don't like to kill nobody. Sammy, he's just an idiot. I'm different. I'm a genuwine son-of-a-bitch from a way back and don't you forget it."

Matt went on past him to Bud's door. He stepped inside and closed the door, discovering that he was shaking as if he were coming down with chills and fever. He fished a match out of his vest pocket, feeling as if he had come into contact with something that was so obscene it was unbearable. He waited until he stopped shaking. Lighting a lamp on the boy's bureau, he turned to the bed and shook Bud awake.

The boy sat up and rubbed his eyes, asking: "Ain't morning yet, is it?"

"No," Matt said. "Get up and dress."

Bud shook his head to clear the cobwebs away, then rubbed his eyes and swung his feet on the floor. Suddenly he seemed to realize something was wrong. He put on his shirt, staring at Matt. He started to button it, asking: "What's up, Pa?"

"All hell broke loose," Matt said. "You won't believe it when I tell you."

As Bud finished dressing, Matt told him as briefly as he could what had happened. Bud listened, his face becoming grave. He was a tall boy, almost as tall as his father, but still gawky and leggy from the rapid growth that often hits a boy in his middle teens. He had been working on the ranch since school was out and had come home the evening before for the celebration. Now Matt wished he had stayed at the ranch.

"What do they want me for?" Bud asked as he tugged on his boots.

"I don't know," Matt answered, "except to say you're a hostage. I feel like hell taking you downstairs, but we've got to play their game for a while."

"I could get through the window," Bud whispered. "You could stay in here and they wouldn't know I was gone. I could have Jerry back here in five minutes."

Matt shook his head. "Bud, believe me about this. There's three of them. They're killers. I know the kind. We've got to take their orders until something happens that gives us a chance. Maybe we'll all get killed playing it safe this way, but I know we'll get killed if we jump them before that something happens. Now, come on."

"You can't let them rob the bank," Bud said.

Matt met the boy's gaze. He said: "I can't let them murder your mother and Jean, either. At first I didn't believe they would, but I do now. Come on, I tell you."

He left the room, Bud following, and went along the hall and down the stairs, ignoring Ross Hart as he passed him.

X

When Matt and Bud reached the bottom of the stairs, Smith motioned for them to sit down. His eyes were thoughtful as he studied Bud. Finally he said: "You're a good-looking boy. It would be a shame for anything to happen to you."

Matt and Bud sat down, neither saying anything. Matt glanced at Nora. Her face was pale, her lips squeezed tightly together. He thought she had control of herself now. If he could gain enough time, he was confident he would find a way to escape this trap in which he and his family found themselves.

Smith was smart, but Matt was certain that sometime within the next twelve hours the outlaws would make a mistake, the fatal kind of mistake that would give him a chance to take them or get word to Jerry Corrigan. Or was this only wishful thinking, the kind of wishful thinking that a man does when he has his back to the wall and is waiting for the firing squad to shoot?

He didn't know. He had worried about Nora's blowing up in a fit of frustration, but he felt better about her now. He glanced at Jean and decided she was the one he had better worry about. She had an expression he had never seen on her face before.

It was as if she had become a little girl again and was having a dream, a wild and terrifying dream that ran on and on endlessly. If she could not grasp the reality of the danger they were in, she, instead of Nora, might be the one to do something foolish that would endanger all of them.

Smith had been studying the faces of the Dugan family, first the women, then Matt, and finally Bud. He said: "I'm a good judge of human nature. I wouldn't be in the business I have followed successfully for ten years if I wasn't. I'm what you good people call a con man, and therefore I live in a sort of twilight zone between the underworld and that of legitimate business. Bank robbing is not in my line, but this looked too good to pass up."

He drew a cigar from his coat pocket and rolled it between his fingers for a while, then he continued: "It's been my experience that women are more reckless than men. That's why I've been concerned about you, Missus Dugan, ever since you tried to jump me when your husband came in."

Irritated, Nora said: "I told you I learned my lesson. I don't know why I have to keep saying it."

"Because this is the only time we will all be together," Smith said. "I want Bud to understand this, too." He turned to the boy. "There is a possibility in this kind of situation that someone will try to be a hero and upset the apple cart and put everyone in danger. I suppose you might defeat our plan, but you'll get yourself killed doing it." He turned back to Matt. "I'm not the kind of gambler who likes a game with the deuces wild. I intend to copper my bet. First, we'll talk about tomorrow. Dugan, I suppose you go to the bank about eight?"

Matt nodded. "I don't have a set time,

but I get there sometime between eight and nine."

"They'll look for you at the usual time in the morning?"

Matt nodded again. "That's right."

"I expect you to go ahead with your regular habits." Smith put the cigar into his mouth and chewed on it a moment, then he said: "Sammy and I may go downtown in the morning and mingle with the crowd. We might even drop into the bank. If we do, you will treat us as if we were your wife's cousins."

"I have to be at the hotel at eight to help make sandwiches," Nora said.

"Keep your date," Smith said. "Just be sure you don't say or do anything to make your friends think something is wrong."

"Jerry Corrigan will probably stop by in the morning," Matt said. "He often does."

"Let him in," Smith said. "Give him a cup of coffee. Act normal. Jean, you will stay in the house until we leave at noon tomorrow. If Corrigan wants you to go to the celebration with him, tell him you have a headache."

"I never have headaches," Jean said.

"You start tomorrow morning," Smith said.

"I'm not going off and leave Jean in the

house with you and Sammy," Nora said sharply. "If you go downtown, she'll be alone with Ross Hart and you say he's a terrible man."

"He's terrible only when you fail to co-operate," Smith said. "Now then, Dugan, I can read your mind. You have been thinking about how you and the sheriff will take us when we leave the house with the *dinero*. You think we will be vulnerable at that time. No, we won't be, because Sammy is taking Bud to a soddy a little ways from town. He will be a prisoner until we're safe. Then he will be released."

"I won't let you," Nora cried. "I'll co-operate here in town and we'll promise not to do anything about capturing you for as long as you say, but I won't let you take Bud and maybe murder him."

Smith looked at her as if suddenly he was very tired. "Missus Dugan, I have gone over this with you until it has become monotonous, and yet you still talk about what you will let us do. All I can tell you is that he will not be murdered if you co-operate, in town and everywhere else." Smith turned to Bud. "This works the other way, too, son. Your folks' safety depends on the way you act. If you make trouble, or manage to escape and spread the word, you will be the cause of at least your sister's death and probably your parents, too."

"I don't aim to make any trouble," Bud said.

"Good." Smith nodded at Sammy Bean. "Take him along."

Sammy motioned for Bud to get up. "Come on, kid. I'm getting a little boogery about this deal, so, if you kick any dust into my face, I'll twist your damn' neck just like I would a rooster for Sunday dinner."

Bud rose. He glanced at his mother who had folded her hands on her lap so tightly the fingers were white, then he looked at Matt. "You're right, Pa. We've got to play their game for a while."

He crossed the room and disappeared into the back of the house. Matt didn't move as he heard the screen door bang shut. Smith had read his mind and read it accurately. He had not fully understood what Smith had meant by saying he was using Bud as a hostage, so he had thought he could play it out until the men left tomorrow noon, then he and Jerry Corrigan could capture them and recover the money.

Now for one long and terrifying moment he pictured Bud lying on his back on the dirt floor of some deserted soddy out in the sandhills, a bullet in his head. Bud was his only son. Nora was young enough to have more children, but she couldn't. The doctor had made that plain enough when Bud was born.

Matt knew, then, in this moment of black despair, that he could not as much as lift a finger to save the dam and ditch project that meant so much to everyone in Amity.

XI

Bud stopped on the back porch when Sammy Bean said: "Wait. You got a lantern around here?"

"There's one hanging beside the door."

"Light it," Sammy said.

Bud took the lantern off the nail, jacked up the chimney, and, scratching a match to life, held the flame to the wick. He blew out the match and eased the chimney back into place. When he looked up, he saw that Sammy was watching him, his right hand on the butt of his gun.

For the first time in his life fear hit Bud so hard that he was sick in the pit of his stomach. He moistened his lips, then he began to tremble. He called himself a fool, but he couldn't control his body.

He'd had several narrow escapes from death. Once he had been caught in a blizzard and had almost frozen before he'd stumbled into a ranch house. Another time, when he was hunting with his father in the mountains, he had wounded a bear that had nearly killed him before he finished the animal.

There were other cases like these, but he had never been one to worry about death. He didn't know why this wild fear hit him the way it did now. Maybe it was the hard, brittle expression on Sammy Bean's face.

Staring at the young outlaw in the murky lantern light, Bud knew beyond the slightest doubt that Sammy could and would kill him if he were given an excuse, that John Smith would kill Jean if anything went wrong tomorrow. This was the one horrible fact that controlled what he did, the outlaws' capacity for murder.

"You're fixing to kill all of us before you're done, ain't you?" Bud whispered.

Sammy Bean laughed. Bud hated him and he hated himself for his weakness. He had not been able to lift his voice above a whisper; he was not able to control his hands, which were shaking. Sammy recognized the fear that possessed Bud. It was probably what amused him.

"Well, now, that depends, kid," Sammy said, "but I'll tell you one thing. If you decide to make a run for it, I'll kill you." He motioned toward the barn. "Go ahead of me and saddle your horse."

Bud stepped off the porch and strode to the shed, Sammy staying two paces behind him. He opened the door and, going inside, hung the lantern on a nail. He saw that three strange horses were in the barn. One, a buckskin, was saddled. Sammy stepped into the stall and tightened the cinch, then backed the buckskin into the runway. He waited while Bud saddled the sorrel.

Bud's fingers were all thumbs and it took him twice as long as usual to saddle the horse. When he finally finished, he led the sorrel outside, Sammy following. He blew out the lantern, closed the door, and turned to Bud who stood waiting, the reins in his hand.

"While we're riding, you're staying beside me," Sammy said. "We'll head a little west of north. If we run into anybody who asks you what you're doing this time of night, tell 'em you're taking a new cowhand to your dad's ranch."

"How did you know our ranch was in this direction?" Bud asked.

"Why, we've been informed," Sammy said. "Now, remember that it don't take me long to get my gun out of leather. The first jump that sorrel makes will get you a slug between the shoulders. Savvy?"

"I savvy, all right," Bud said in a low tone.

"Then let's ride," Sammy said.

Bud stepped into the saddle and rode down the alley beside Sammy to the street that ran north and south along the west edge of the courthouse block. In the moonlight the platform from which the governor would speak tomorrow looked like a gallows, or so it seemed to Bud.

A moment later they were out of town and riding up the gentle slope that lay north of Buffalo Creek. The road to Burlington was somewhere to the west. Bud glanced at Sammy and saw that his right hand was resting on the butt of his gun. He looked straight ahead at the long rise in front of him and felt the icy prickles race down his spine.

Once more fear took possession of Bud so completely that it was all he could do to keep from digging his heels into the flanks of his sorrel and making a wild dash through the sagebrush. The wind that raced across the prairie was hot, but Bud was actually chilled.

A soddy loomed ahead of them. Sammy said: "Here we are." He reined up and whistled twice. Suddenly Bud realized where they were. This was Uncle Pete Fisher's soddy. He had built it years ago when he'd first proved up on his homestead. He still owned the land and kept the soddy in livable condition. He stayed in town most of the time, coming out here to spend a night when, as he put it, he needed to hear the coyotes howl and feel the wind in his face.

Most folks said he wanted to get away from his overbearing wife once in a while. This was the only property he had left after he lost the bank, and, although the land was practically worthless, it was his.

Bud's dad thought that the reason the old man came out here was to stand on land that belonged to him. He had told Matt that, when he was in town, he guessed that even the air he breathed belonged to his wife.

Bud had heard all of this from his father more than once. Now the notion struck him that Uncle Pete must have been the one who had planned the whole thing. After being the most important man in the county for years and then losing everything except this quarter-section of range land, he must have gone crazy and thought up this scheme for robbing the bank without being involved personally.

"So it was Uncle Pete," Bud said.

"Who's Uncle Pete?" Sammy asked.

"Pete Fisher," Bud answered. "He owns this soddy."

Sammy laughed softly. "Sure, Fisher is the one." He whistled again.

This time the door opened and a woman stepped outside, a shotgun in her hand. "I see you got him," she said.

"Get down," Sammy said. "I'll put your horse in the shed. This is where you stay till noon tomorrow."

When Bud was inside the soddy, he saw that the windows were covered by blankets. The woman pulled the door shut, the shotgun still in her hands. She was a big woman, not fat, but raw-boned and muscular. Bud guessed she was as strong as the average man. She wore high-heeled boots, a dark green riding skirt, and a tan blouse. Her blonde hair was pinned on the back of her head. She was clean, and right now at least she seemed pleasant enough.

"Sit down, kid," she said, and motioned to one of the straight-backed chairs. "Surprised that a woman is gonna run herd on you?"

He nodded. "A lot of things are surprising me."

She laughed. "I'll bet they are, kid. I'll bet

they are." Her face turned grave as she bit her lip and stared at him for a moment, her good-natured expression gone. "We'd best have an understanding, kid. Don't figure you can take advantage of me. I'm tougher'n a boot heel. If you get ornery, I'll blow your head off. Savvy?"

"I sure do," Bud said. "That's about all I've been hearing."

"I guess all of us want you to know that, when we talk, we ain't just making the wind blow," she said. "You and your family got caught in this scheme. None of us, unless it's Ross Hart, wants to hurt you. But on the other hand, we can hurt you plenty if something goes wrong that might make us lose our big, fat fee."

He started to ask her what she meant by big, fat fee. It didn't seem right for her to call the stolen bank money a fee. Sammy came in then and closed the door, so Bud didn't ask the question.

The woman went to Sammy and kissed him, then patted his cheek and said something that must have been a love word. It seemed a little crazy to Bud. She was older than Sammy. Besides that, two people working on a bank-robbing scheme like this didn't seem to be the kind who would be lovers. But then, maybe all lovers didn't look like Jean and Jerry.

"It's going fine so far," Sammy said. "The Dugans are behaving all right. John's a real slick one. He even fooled the sheriff when he came in with the Dugan girl."

"I ain't staying here for no posse to find," the woman warned. "You be sure John Smith knows that."

"Oh, he knows it, all right," Sammy said. "No reason why it won't work on schedule just like we planned. Well, I've got to get back. Don't let the kid get the bulge on you."

"He won't," the woman said.

She kissed Sammy again. After he left, she barred the door, then jerked a thumb at the bunk. "You lie down and go to sleep. After a while I may lie down with you, but right now I'm wide awake, thinking about all that *dinero* Sammy's gonna make out of this caper."

"What are you getting a big, fat fee for?" Bud asked.

"For murdering. . . ." She stopped, looking as guilty as if she were a small child caught with her hand in the cookie jar. "You little bastard, you ask too many questions. Now, you go to sleep or, by God, I'll put you to sleep."

He didn't argue. She looked mean, real

mean. He lay on his back, staring at the ceiling, the familiar prickles running up and down his back again. Who were they going to murder? Not his father. They'd had plenty of chance to do that already. And not Jerry Corrigan. They'd have made him stay when they'd had a chance. No, it must be somebody else, maybe some of the visitors who would be in town for the celebration.

He couldn't think who it would be, and presently he dropped off to sleep, the question still unanswered.

XII

Time dragged for Matt until he began to wonder if Bud and Sammy Bean were going to spend the night on the back porch. He heard nothing for what seemed a long time after the screen slammed shut, then the mutter of talk. After that there was silence again. They must have gone. He relaxed, realizing only then how tense he had been.

Smith rose. "You can't see Ross up there at the head of the stairs, but he can see you. Don't move till I get back."

He left the room and disappeared into the kitchen. Matt glanced at Nora, then at Jean. He said: "This is really happening, Jean."

She had been staring at the floor, her hands clasped on her lap. Now she looked up, whispering: "I'm not sure it is. I never felt like this before in my whole life except when I've had some awful dream. Maybe I'm having one now. I hope I'm alive tomorrow noon so I can wake up from it."

"We will if we don't lose our heads," Matt said, trying to make his voice hold a calm assurance he did not feel.

Smith came back into the room. "They're gone. Sammy should be back in an hour or so. If you folks have kept your heads as Dugan was just saying, the boy will be released about noon tomorrow, unharmed. Now you can go to bed. Jean, you will stay in your room in the morning until you're called. Missus Dugan, you will get breakfast for us. I want a good meal because we'll have to ride like hell when we leave here and I don't know when we'll get a chance to eat again."

"Aren't you afraid I'll poison you?" Nora asked.

Smith's lips smiled, but his bright eyes narrowed and grew hard. "No, I'm not afraid. You'd better make sure I don't get a stomach ache, though. I might lose my temper if I do." He turned to Jean. "Go to bed."

She rose and climbed the stairs and walked past Ross Hart without as much as glancing at him. When her bedroom door slammed shut, Smith said: "Now you old folks can go to bed." His lips widened into his humorless grin again, then it faded. "I guess I'm older than either of you, but tonight you probably feel older than I do. I doubt that you'll sleep much. You'll lie awake and think up a dozen notions to whip us. Slipping out through the window and going after the sheriff, for instance, but you'll give them up."

Nora held up her hands to Matt who stood in front of her. He helped her to her feet. She remained motionless for a moment, staring past him at Smith. She was not a woman who normally hated anyone, but now Matt saw a loathing in her eyes he had never seen there before.

"Before this is over with," she said, "we'll see you dead. I don't know when or how, but we will."

She turned and stalked into the bedroom, her heels *clicking* sharply on the floor. Smith said somberly: "She will be the death of you and your children if you don't talk some sense into her."

Matt followed her into the bedroom and shut the door. She had lighted a lamp on the bureau and now walked to the windows and pulled down the blinds. When she turned, he saw the pulse throbbing in her temples.

"I believe you would give your life to get the best of them," he said.

"Of course I would," she said, "if it would do any good."

"That's the point," he said. "My head still hurts, but I'm thinking straight enough. They're after our money. All right, we'll let them have it and then try to catch up with them after they've left, when you and Jean and Bud are safe."

She started to unbutton her blouse, then dropped her hand. "I'm not going to undress. Something might happen." She sat down on the bed and took off her shoes, and then lay down, frowning at him. "Matt, I don't think we can trust them to do what they say. We don't know they won't kill us after they get the money. We don't know what will happen to Jean when she's alone with them in the morning. We don't know that they'll leave Bud alive when they go."

He sat down on the edge of the bed and tugged off his boots. Then he looked at her. She shocked him. In twenty years of married life he had never seen her like this. But then they had never faced a situation like this before.

"You're saying we had better let them kill us if that will keep them from getting the money?" he asked.

"Maybe," she said. "I don't know. I'm thinking they'll kill us anyway. If that's what we're up against, we'd better deal the cards ourselves."

"What do you mean?"

"The window's open," she said. "Go get Jerry."

He shook his head. "I'd live maybe. You might. Jean wouldn't. Neither would Bud."

"You're going to let them have both the money and our lives?" she asked. "After all you've gone through to raise that ten thousand dollars to do something for Amity?"

"I'd rather let them have the money than to get any of us killed," he answered. "There's a chance we could get the money back, but we'd never get our lives back if they killed us. They're not bluffing, Nora. If we push them, they'll do exactly what they said they would."

He lay down beside her. The room was like an oven. The sweat oozed out of his pores and soaked his clothes. He stared at the ceiling, thinking it wasn't entirely the heat that was making him sweat. He wanted to take his clothes off, but Nora was right.

Something might happen. They had better be dressed.

Nora got up and blew out the lamp, then returned to the bed and lay down. He put a hand on her stomach. It was as tight as a drumhead. His touch was all it took to break her self-control. She began to cry. She turned to him and hugged him. He felt her tears on his cheek; he heard her whisper: "What are we going to do?"

He slipped an arm under her shoulders and brought her body against his. He held her that way for a moment until they made each other so hot that neither could stand it. He kissed her and pulled his arm away from her. She turned to lie on her back again.

"We'll play it out," he said. "We wait for them to make a mistake. Somewhere . . . sometime . . . they'll make one. I'm sure of it."

"Honey, have you thought of what people will say?" she asked. "About you if these . . . these devils get the money and escape? I mean, their staying in our house and you bringing it to them?"

"Yes, I've thought about it," he said somberly. "We'll pay everybody back. With prices what they are now, it would break us if we have to sell the ranch and all our stock,

191

but if we have to start over, it will be better than losing our children."

"I know you're right," she said in a low tone. "I never knew you to be wrong in any kind of a crisis, but I just can't stand it to let these monsters get away with that money after they've come into our house and ordered us around and slugged you. I never thought I would want to kill another human being, but I want to kill these men, all three of them."

He was silent and presently he heard her relaxed breathing and knew she was asleep. He stayed awake. Smith had been right. One idea after another occurred to him, but none would work as long as they had Bud.

He wondered who was involved who lived here in Amity. Someone had to be. Smith had been informed, informed of so many details about Matt and his family that this someone, whoever he was, must be a person who knew the Dugans very well.

Matt went over in his mind each man who might be an informer. Jerry Corrigan? Ridiculous. He was going to marry Jean. Matt had known him since he was a boy and he had never suspected Jerry of doing anything that even smacked of dishonesty. In any case, Jerry would not be involved in a crime that put Jean in danger and she was surely in danger now.

Uncle Pete Fisher? No, that was almost as ridiculous. He was a bitter old man, as he had admitted, and there were some folks in town who thought he was a little foolish, sitting on a bench in front of the courthouse and telling tall tales to the town boys like Bud the way he did.

There were plenty of others who were better bets. The hotel man, Cole Talbot, was one. His business had been next to nothing ever since the panic had struck almost a year ago. His temper had grown worse until he seemed to be mad at everyone and everything.

Fred Follett, the cashier? Matt was fond of him, but he had to admit Follett was a good candidate. He knew the $10,000 had been delivered to the bank, a fact which Matt had not advertised. He was a poor man who wanted to marry a girl who had a bad case of the gimmes. A portion of the $10,000 would set him up with the girl.

There were plenty of other men in town who knew the Dugan habits well enough to give Smith all the information he needed. The saloon man, Sam Elliott. Walt Payson, who owned the livery stable. Jim Long, who ran the Mercantile and was in bad financial trouble.

Too, it could be one or more of the cattle-men. Some had opposed the dam project on general principles, claiming that it was a bad thing for any cattle country to start inviting farmers to come in and settle. The next thing you knew, they said, farmers would be stupid enough to start dry farming and there went your range.

It didn't seem to Matt that any of these men would be part of a scheme that would endanger Nora and Jean. Even Fred Follett. . . . Matt tensed. He heard voices from the front of the house. One of them belonged to Jerry Corrigan.

XIII

Jerry Corrigan woke with a start. He was sitting up in bed, the words Ross Hart running through his mind like an ugly refrain. The name had been vaguely familiar when he heard it. Now he had to identify it because it was significant. He didn't know why, but he knew it was.

He had not been asleep very long. The moonlight was falling through the window just as it had when he'd gone to bed. He put his feet on the floor, knowing he had to do something. To go to the Dugan house and knock on the door at this time of night

194

and get them up just to ask about a man they didn't even know was ridiculous.

But he had to do something. *Ross Hart. Ross Hart. Ross Hart.* On occasion he'd had a tune run through his mind like that. Sometimes he wouldn't get rid of it for hours and it would almost drive him crazy.

Usually it was a tune that meant something. Maybe Jean had hummed it when they'd been together, or she might have played it on the piano. Perhaps they had been to a band concert in the park and the band had played it. He had a hunch that the name Ross Hart meant something that had to do with Jean's safety.

He dressed, thinking that this last notion was as ridiculous as getting the Dugans out of bed. Jean was safely home with her parents, her brother, and two cousins. What could a strange man named Ross Hart do to her? He buckled his gun belt around him, upset because of the vague uneasiness that refused to go away.

He went down the stairs and across the deserted lobby and into the street. He had never felt this way in his life before. It was like seeing some sort of apparition that you can't identify. You know it isn't real, but you have chills running up and down your back because it is something strange and mysterious that you don't understand.

Corrigan turned toward the courthouse, thinking that he might have seen the name on a Reward dodger sometime or other, perhaps months ago. He had forgotten it, but perhaps the memory had lingered in some dark corner of his mind to pop out after he had gone to sleep.

This seemed ridiculous, too. At least it had never happened before, but that didn't mean it couldn't happen now. A good many things were taking place in the next month that would make it the most important month in his life. By the time he reached the front door of the courthouse, he decided that he was just plain nervous about getting married. Well, he was here, so he'd go ahead and look through the Reward dodgers.

He felt his way along the dark corridor to his office at the end of the hall, his footsteps making weird, echoing sounds in the nearly empty building. He scratched a match and lighted a bracket lamp on the wall above the desk, then sat down and took a pile of Reward dodgers from the bottom drawer.

He began thumbing through the notices. He had almost reached the bottom of the stack when he found the one he wanted. It had come in nearly a year ago. He had not paid much attention to it because it was from southern Arizona and he had no reason to think that Ross Hart would ever show up here in eastern Colorado.

As he read, Corrigan understood why he had not entirely forgotten the name. Ross Hart was about as bad as they came. He was young, only twenty when the Reward dodger had been printed, but if he lived, he would become as famous as Jesse or Frank James or one of the Daltons or maybe Sam Bass.

According to the description, he was a small man with red hair and brown eyes. He was fast and deadly with the two six-shooters he habitually carried. He was wanted for bank robbery, stage robbery, and murder. No one knew how many women and men he had killed, but it was thought to be at least ten.

After the last stage hold-up, he was known to have fled into Mexico and had not been heard of since. A reward of $1,000 was offered for his capture, dead or alive. At the bottom of the paper were the words in tall letters: **THIS MAN IS DANGEROUS.**

Corrigan sat back and wiped the sweat from his face. How could Nora's cousins get hooked up with a man like that? But maybe he was jumping at shadows. This probably wasn't the same Ross Hart. An outlaw as notorious as he was would surely change his name.

Corrigan rolled and lighted a cigarette, then leaned back in his swivel chair. He stared at the ceiling and tried to think this through. Where had the real Ross Hart spent the last year? The Reward dodger said he made a habit of jumping back and forth across the border, but Corrigan thought he would have heard of him sometime during the past year if he had come back into the United States.

Ross Hart was not a common name like John Smith. Corrigan supposed there were 10,000 John Smiths in the United States, but there were not likely to be many Ross Harts, particularly in the West and be the kind of men who could hire out as cowhands. This last thought finally forced Corrigan's decision. Ross Hart might have decided that the heat was so great he'd better just lie low somewhere. Riding for a cattle buyer in the Grand Junction area was about as safe a hide-out as he would be likely to find.

Corrigan dropped the Reward dodgers back into the drawer, closed it, blew out the lamp, and left the office. He was bothered by the fact that Ross Hart had not changed his name, but it didn't prove anything. Men like Hart sometimes kept their real names simply as an act of bravado. Too, he may have thought it wouldn't make any difference, that law officers in Colorado wouldn't know anything about him.

Matt would more than likely cuss him out for waking him in the middle of the night, tired as he was and with a big day coming up tomorrow. But he was going to do it anyway. All of his thinking about the real outlaw and this cowboy in the Dugan house had been wild guessing. Corrigan had no way of knowing what was in the outlaw's mind as to why he would hide out up in Colorado or why he didn't change his name. But he did know a little bit about what the outlaw looked like and his approximate age.

If this man tallied, Corrigan would jail him, dangerous or not. The chances were that John Smith and Sammy Bean didn't know anything about the fellow's record. Naturally Smith wouldn't quiz him about where he had been or why he was looking for work on the Grand. The only thing Smith would want to know was whether he could handle a riding job.

He reached the Dugan gate, opened it, and cursed softly when it *squealed* loudly enough to wake everyone in the house. He walked up the path, aware that someone was standing on the front porch. He smelled cigar smoke, and, when he reached the steps, he saw the red glow of the cigar.

"Who is it?" the man asked.

Corrigan dropped his right hand to the butt of his gun, suddenly realizing that if this was Ross Hart, he might be a dead man in another second. He stood there, looking up, not saying anything for a moment. He tried to make out the man's shape, but he remained back in the shadows. The voice was familiar, so it wouldn't be Hart's. Corrigan hadn't seen or heard him. This must be John Smith. He didn't sound the way Corrigan remembered Sammy Bean's voice.

"Say, you're the sheriff, aren't you?" the man on the porch asked as he stepped down into the moonlight. "I didn't recognize you. A man just naturally looks different in the moonlight than he does inside the house in the lamplight."

Corrigan sighed in relief. It was John Smith. He said: "I didn't recognize you, either, standing back there in the shadows."

"Sorry." Smith laughed softly. "After all, I'm a visitor and I'm not familiar with the local custom of the sheriff calling on his sweetheart in the middle of the night."

Smith was needling him and he didn't like

it. He hesitated a moment, not wanting a row with the man, and then he began to wonder why Smith wasn't asleep. He decided he might just as well ask straight out.

"How do you happen to be awake?"

"Not that it's the sheriff's business," Smith said, "but it was so hot in the house I couldn't sleep." He hesitated, then added: "To tell the truth, I've been more worried than I cared to tell Nora. I had hoped to borrow money from the bank, but Matt was saying his bank is in pretty deep financing this dam project, so I didn't even ask him. I just haven't made a damned nickel since the panic hit last fall. That's why I came over here. I thought cattle might be cheaper than they are on the Grand."

"I see," Corrigan said, thinking it sounded logical enough. "I want to see Matt. I'll go on in and wake him."

"Oh, I wouldn't do that," Smith said. "Matt needs all the sleep he can get."

"I know that," Corrigan said, "but this is important. I've got to see him."

"Why don't you tell me what it is?" Smith said. "I'll pass it along as soon as he gets up in the morning."

This wasn't right, Corrigan thought. He was a lot closer to Matt Dugan than this cousin of Nora's who happened to drift in to spend the night. Why should Smith not want him to talk to Matt? Corrigan tried to stay calm, to tell himself that he was just boogery over all the things that had happened and would happen tomorrow, and the things that might happen. Anyhow, he was sleepy and tired. He wasn't going to stand here all night arguing with John Smith.

"I'll wake him," Corrigan said.

"No, I will," Smith said, and swung around and disappeared into the house.

Corrigan knew it wasn't right at all. The notion worked into his mind that John Smith and Ross Hart might be in cahoots on something that wasn't open and above board. Sure, it was ridiculous, and it would be stupid to push too hard tonight. Maybe Matt wouldn't want to tell him and maybe he didn't know that something was up.

He waited, deciding he'd wait till morning, but he heard Matt and Smith cross the front room to the porch, and Smith saying: "There he is, Matt. I told him you needed sleep, but he was bound to get you up."

"It's all right," Matt said, and stepped down off the porch. "What's on your mind, Jerry?"

Smith remained on the porch not more than fifteen feet away. Corrigan lowered his voice, asking: "What does this man Ross Hart look like?" He had an idea Smith heard, but he'd have to whisper into Matt's ear to keep him from hearing. Maybe it was just as well that Smith knew he was suspicious.

"I haven't seen him real good," Matt said. "He's been upstairs ever since I got home, but I went up to Bud's room and he was in the hall. He's a big man, real dark. Maybe thirty years old."

Corrigan took a long breath that was almost a sob. He had never felt so relieved in his life. He said: "I guess he couldn't be about twenty-one, red-headed, and small?"

"Hell, no," Matt said. "I saw him well enough to be sure he didn't look like that."

"I'm sorry I woke you up," Corrigan said. "Go back to bed."

He wheeled and strode down the path.

Matt called: "What was eating on you, Jerry?"

"A mistake," Corrigan said. "Tell Jean I'll see her early in the morning."

He went on, walking fast, but after he was back in bed in his hotel room, he couldn't go to sleep. He was relieved to know that Ross Hart was not the outlaw Ross Hart, but actually he was more disturbed than ever because now he had a hunch that there was something false about John Smith. He'd find out from Jean in the morning.

XIV

Corrigan slept very little that night. He dropped off sometime before dawn, then woke an hour or so later. The sun wasn't up yet, but it would be in a matter of minutes. He couldn't get breakfast at this hour, so he lay on his back and stared at the ceiling as the dawn light steadily deepened.

He couldn't go back to sleep. This was the biggest day in the history of Amity and he didn't want anything to go wrong, for his own sake as well as that of the community. For Matt's sake, too.

He thought about the governor and wondered if he would be in any real danger after he arrived. In any case, it was too late to stop him now. All that Corrigan could do was to keep moving through the crowd, keep his eyes open, and watch for anything that might be a threat to the governor's life.

Corrigan decided he would turn the Owl Creek men loose after he had breakfast and tell them to get out of town and stay out. He'd need the cell space for drunks by evening and he didn't think the threats he'd heard the night before were serious. Then his mind completed the circle and returned to John Smith and Ross Hart, but he still had no answer, just the question.

No use to stay in bed any longer. The lumpy mattress had become unbearable. He put his feet on the floor and rubbed his eyes. They felt as gritty as if they were full of sand. He shaved in cold water, the uneasiness in him growing. A phony John Smith who claimed to be a relative and a man with an outlaw's name staying the night in the Dugan house was enough to make a man uneasy.

He strapped his gun belt around his waist, put his hat on his head, and went downstairs to the dining room that had just been opened. No one else was there. Folks had celebrated too much the night before to get up early, he thought. When he finished eating, he left the dining room and crossed the lobby to the street, which was deserted at this hour.

He turned toward the courthouse, thinking that the town would be jumping within an hour or so. For the first time since he had pinned on the star, he wished he had a dozen deputies to patrol the town, particularly the area around the courthouse where the crowd would soon be gathering. But he didn't have even one deputy.

What happened this day would be Jerry Corrigan's responsibility no matter what kind of tragedy took place or how it came about. If he wanted to see Jean this morning, he'd better do it now or he'd be so busy he wouldn't see her all day.

The day would be another scorcher, he told himself as he turned into the courthouse. Even inside the building the air had cooled very little during the night. Outside the burning sun would add to people's tempers. If the governor said the wrong thing, with folks feeling the way they did. . . . Then he told himself that nothing bad was going to happen. Not today. He wouldn't let it.

He unlocked the big cell that held the cowboys he had jailed for drunkenness or disturbing the peace and told them they could go, then advised them to behave themselves. This was a big day for the entire county and he didn't want any more trouble. They promised they'd be on their best behavior and scurried out of the courthouse as if afraid Corrigan might change his mind and lock them up again.

After they were gone, he turned back to the cell that held the Owl Creek men. He stared at them through the bars, wondering if he should keep them locked up. They were the meanest-looking trio he had ever seen in his life, and his conviction that the threats they'd made the night before weren't serious began to waver.

"The snot-nosed sheriff is back, boys," Vance Yarnell said. "Ain't he an ugly devil?"

"He sure is," Harry Mason agreed. "I don't see how he can stand hisself."

"Ugly ain't the right word," Zach Lupton said. "He's wearing a mask, ain't he? That can't be his real face."

This kind of hoorawing was typical of them. He decided again that their tough talk last night had been the whiskey talking and had not meant anything. He'd let them out and start the day with an empty jail.

"I'm laughing," Corrigan said as he unlocked the cell. "Now I'm going to tell you a joke, but it ain't funny. Not even a little bit. You boys get on your horses and ride out of town and stay out all day. I'll give you fifteen minutes. If I see any of you after that fifteen minutes is up, I'll throw you back into that cell and I'll lose the key."

"That's a joke?" Yarnell asked as he followed Corrigan along the corridor into his office. "If it is, it ain't funny, for a fact." He took his gun belt that Corrigan handed to him and strapped it around his waist, then he asked: "What did you hit me with last night? Zach and Harry claims it was your fist, but I know damned well they're lying. Nobody could hit me that hard with just a fist."

"Come on." Mason was already through the door. "Vance, ain't you had a belly full of this stinking hole?"

"More'n enough," Yarnell said bitterly. "That star-toter will never get me in there again."

Yarnell followed Mason and Lupton out of the courthouse. Corrigan watched from the window of his office until they rode out of town. He still wondered if he had done right turning them loose, but he wouldn't know the answer for sure until the governor had made his speech and was safely back on the train at Burlington.

He had known the Owl Creek men for a long time. They were a no-good lot, but they had never made any trouble worse than getting drunk and fighting and making nuisances out of themselves. He hoped they'd take his advice and stay out of town and he thought they would.

As he left the courthouse and turned toward the Dugan house, he heard someone call: "Jerry! Wait a minute, Jerry. I want to talk to you."

Corrigan turned and swore softly. Uncle

Pete Fisher was hurrying toward him as fast as he could make his rheumatic body move. He was the last man in town Corrigan wanted to talk to. He'd had enough of him last night.

He couldn't handle the old man in the rough way he'd handled the Owl Creek bunch. Fisher was almost a legend in the community. He had done a great deal for the town and the county in his time, and he deserved respect, but it was difficult to respect a man who had become as crotchety and perverse as he was.

Now, watching Fisher as he approached, Corrigan realized he was a little drunk. That was surprising this early in the morning, but far more surprising was the fact that his beard and mustache were white with just a trace of black shoe polish or dye or whatever he used.

"I've got to talk to you." Fisher placed his gnarled hands on Corrigan's wide shoulders and gripped them as hard as he could, his whiskey-sour breath turning Corrigan's stomach. "You've got to do something. You've got to keep the governor out of Amity. I don't know how you can do it, but you can figure something out."

Corrigan jerked free of Fisher's grip and stepped back. "Uncle Pete, you'd better go to bed. I'll bet you haven't slept any all night."

"By glory, that's right," Fisher said. "You know I hate that damned Ben Wyatt for what he's done to me and my town and the whole state of Colorado, but I don't want anything to happen that will hurt Amity. That's why I ain't slept, and it's why I'm telling you that you've got to do something . . . anything . . . to keep him out of town."

"I just turned the Owl Creek bunch loose," Corrigan said. "Are you trying to tell me I should have kept 'em in jail?"

"No, no, no." Fisher wiped a hand across his eyes. "Everything will be all right if you keep Wyatt from making his speech. You've got to keep him out of town. That's all. Just turn him around and head him back to the railroad."

Fisher was almost crying. The corners of his mouth were trembling and his voice was barely audible. Corrigan backed up another step, not wanting to quarrel with Fisher, but he didn't have all morning to stand here and argue with an old man who had lost every nickel he had and, blaming the governor for it, hated him with a passion that was almost insanity.

"Look, Uncle Pete," Corrigan said, "I've got to run over to Matt's house. I want to see Jean a minute before the shebang starts. I'd like to oblige you, but this has gone too far. There's nothing I can do to keep Wyatt out of town."

Fisher began to shake. He tried to say something, but the words wouldn't come for a time. Finally he blurted: "Damn it, Jerry, when a man makes a mistake . . . I mean, there must be some way to stop. . . ."

His throat seemed to close up and he wiped a hand across his eyes again. Then he had control of himself. He hurried on: "Jerry, you're the only man I can turn to. Matt won't do anything. Seems like nobody will even listen to me. I reckon I've had a drink or two more'n I should, and I know I'm old and I don't amount to much any more, but I know what I'm talking about. You've got to keep Ben Wyatt off that platform. If you don't, you'll be sorry as long as you live."

"Uncle Pete, this is going to be a long day," Corrigan said kindly. "Now, why don't you go home and get a little sleep, and then, when you wake up, take care of your beard and mustache. I guess you're awful worried about something because they've turned white in just the last few hours."

"No," Fisher said sharply. "It's going to stay white from now on. I'm tired of trying to be something I'm not. All right, you go see your girl, but you think about what I've told you. Talk to Matt about it. Between you, I guess, you can think of some way to stop Wyatt."

"I'll think about it," Corrigan said.

Turning from Fisher, he strode away toward the Dugan house. He wondered what had changed the old man. He hadn't talked this way last night. Then Corrigan put Fisher out of his mind. He had greater worries than the warnings of an old ex-banker who was just drunk enough to kick up a cloud of dust trying to keep a man he hated out of town.

XV

Matt Dugan did not sleep during the long night. He'd had his share of worries as a husband, a father, a rancher, a lawman, and finally as a banker, but in his active and sometimes turbulent life he had never had to face anything like this. He felt helpless. That was a new feeling and one he didn't like.

The bedroom did not cool much during the night even with the windows open. By the time it was daylight he felt as if the last bit of oxygen in the room had been used.

He had to get out of here and into some other part of the house.

Nora was still sleeping. She lay on her back breathing regularly, her mouth slightly open. He slipped out of bed, being careful not to wake her, and, picking up his boots, tiptoed out of the bedroom.

Sammy Bean was sprawled out on the couch, snoring loudly, his parted lips fluttering with each breath. Ross Hart had called him an idiot, and now with a vacant expression on his face he looked like one. Smith sat in a chair across the room from Bean, his eyes as bright and sharp as they had been the night before.

Matt sat down on a chair and pulled on his boots. Smith smiled and said pleasantly: "Good morning. Did you sleep well?"

"No," Matt answered.

He got up and went into the kitchen, expecting Smith to follow him. He built a fire in the range and filled the teakettle and set it on the front of the stove. Smith didn't appear. Matt made coffee, filled the wash basin, and scrubbed his face and hands and combed his hair, but still Smith did not leave the front room.

He didn't need to, Matt thought bitterly. Nora was in the bedroom. Jean was asleep upstairs. Bud was being held as a hostage.

Sure, Matt could walk right out through the back door and go after a gun or he could fetch Jerry Corrigan and a dozen other men; he could prevent the money in the bank from being stolen and thus save the dam. All three outlaws would be killed or captured, and in the process Matt would lose everyone in his family.

Matt stood beside the range, listening to the wood *snap* and *pop.* He had told Nora they would play it out, and now, hours later, he knew that nothing had changed. It was still the only thing they could do. He filled the firebox with coal and set the scuttle on the floor, and then he was aware that Smith was standing in the doorway.

"Is your wife asleep?" Smith asked. "Or is she reluctant to wait on her guests under the circumstances?"

"She was asleep when I got up," Matt said.

"Wake her," Smith said. "We want our breakfast. You want yours, too. You'll soon be going about your business as usual. Don't forget that for a minute."

Smith stepped back and Matt walked through the door and went on into the bedroom, his pulse pounding in his temples. It would help relieve his tension if he gave Smith a verbal cursing, but that was a luxury he could not afford. *Play it out,* he told himself again. *Wait for them to make a mistake. Don't do anything to make the situation worse.*

Nora woke when he came into the room. She didn't move or speak. She looked at him, her eyes questioning. He said: "I built the fire and started the coffee. Smith wants you to get up and cook breakfast. I guess it's time. I have to get to the bank and you have to be at the Methodist church at eight to help Hannah Talbot make sandwiches."

Nora got up. She didn't say anything as she turned to the bureau and started brushing her hair. Matt watched her a moment, sensing that she was close to the breaking point. He wasn't sure she could hold up through these next five or six hours, listening to the excited chatter of a dozen women while they made sandwiches and not be able to do or say anything that would give away their secret. That was up to her. He would have his own problem trying to carry on the bank's business.

He left the bedroom, closing the door behind him. Sammy Bean was sitting up on the couch, yawning loudly and rubbing his eyes. Matt said to Smith: "She'll be along in a minute."

He went into the kitchen, found that the water in the teakettle was hot, and decided he had better shave. He'd get out of the house as soon as breakfast was over. Everyone would be safer if that were the case. He realized that his nerves were tightening and that he was about as close to losing his self-control as Nora was.

His right hand, which held the razor, was shaky and he nicked himself on the cheek. By the time he finished shaving and had washed the lather from his face, the bleeding had stopped. Nora came into the kitchen, glanced at him, and opened her mouth to say something, then closed it and went on into the pantry. Smith stood in the doorway watching, smiling as if he found this an amusing situation.

"Get the girl up," Smith said. "I want her dressed and ready to entertain the sheriff if he comes in."

Matt nodded and went upstairs. Ross Hart was not in sight. He was probably still in bed in Nora's sewing room. Matt opened Jean's door and stepped into her room. She woke at once, startled, and sat up. Seeing who it was, she sighed and rubbed her eyes.

"Are they still here?" she whispered.

"They're still here," Matt said. "The next four or five hours will be the hard ones. Smith wants you to get dressed and come downstairs. You'll have to entertain Jerry if he stops, and he probably will."

Matt hesitated, thinking about Corrigan's temper. If he caught on to what was happening, he'd blow everything wide open. He added: "You've got to fool Jerry into thinking that nothing's wrong. It'll take the best job of acting you ever did."

She nodded. "I'll do the best I can, but you know how Jerry is."

"Yes, I know," Matt said.

He returned to the kitchen. Nora was frying bacon and eggs, and making toast in the oven. When they were done, she said: "Butter the toast, will you, Matt?"

He nodded. As soon as he finished, Smith said: "Put Ross Hart's breakfast on a plate. He's staying upstairs. Sammy will take it to him."

Nora obeyed and Sammy Bean left the kitchen with the plate and a cup of coffee. Nora motioned toward the table. "Sit down," she said.

"Aren't you going to eat with us, Missus Dugan?" Smith asked with feigned solicitude.

"A cup of coffee is all I want," Nora said.

She poured her coffee and stood at the stove, sipping it, her gaze on Smith as if he had hypnotized her. Smith laughed softly as he sat down and filled his plate. He said: "I hope it's not my company that blunted your appetite, Missus Dugan. You would find me quite charming if you gave me a chance."

"I've read that in Ceylon they make pets out of cobras," Nora said, "but I wouldn't do it."

Smith frowned. Matt kept on eating, but he covertly watched the outlaw. He wished Nora would keep her mouth shut. There was nothing to be gained by insulting Smith and for a moment Matt thought the man was going to take Nora's remark as an insult. Then he shrugged and smiled.

"I believe she's complimenting me," Smith said. "A cobra is dangerous, so I assume Missus Dugan is aware that I am dangerous." He reached for the toast, glancing at Nora, then he brought his gaze to Matt. "See to it that your sheriff doesn't hang around here all morning. If he hasn't showed up by the time you leave, tell your girl."

"He won't stay," Matt said. "He'll have plenty to do downtown and around the courthouse."

He hesitated, thinking of a question that had been in and out of his mind from the time Jerry Corrigan had got him out of bed during the night. Smith probably wouldn't answer it, but he decided to ask anyway.

"What was bothering Corrigan last night when he asked me about Ross Hart? Does he know anything about Hart?"

Smith grinned. "Sure he does. At least the name meant something to him. You see, the real Ross Hart was twenty-one, he was small and red-headed, and he was a killer. I suppose your young sheriff either remembered that much about him or he went through his Reward dodgers and read his description. The man upstairs is not really Ross Hart, but we'll call him that. Not that it makes any difference, but his first name is Ross."

"I don't savvy," Matt said. "Why did you pick that name?"

"The real Ross Hart was killed a few days ago in a gunfight in Nogales," Smith said, "but it wasn't in the papers, so I was sure nobody up here would have heard about it. The idea was that you and your family would recognize the name and be properly intimidated." Smith grinned wryly. "I was wrong. The name didn't mean a damned thing to any of you, so it wasn't a good idea, after all."

Matt rose as Jean came into the kitchen. He said: "I'd better get along to the bank."

"Yes, I think you had," Smith agreed. "I've got one more thing to tell you. I want your daughter to hear it, too. The man upstairs is as much of a killer as the real Ross Hart. Don't let what I told you change anything." He nodded at Jean. "He would kill a woman as soon as he would a man."

"Damn it," Matt shouted, "have you got to keep piling it on? We'll play your game and we'll go on playing it until we get a chance. . . ."

He stopped and took a long breath. Smith was baiting him, he thought, and he had let his temper run away with him for a few seconds. All he had done was to give Smith a little satisfaction.

"You won't get a chance at anything, Dugan," Smith said, smiling again. "We do have to keep piling it on. We don't want you to forget, not for even one small part of a minute."

Matt turned to Nora. "You ready to go?"

Nora was looking at Jean. Smith nodded as if he understood. "She'll be quite safe, Missus Dugan, as long as you remember what your husband said about playing the game."

"I couldn't forget if I tried," Nora said, and, snatching an apron off a nail behind the stove, ran out of the room.

Matt caught up with her in the hall. She stopped to wait for him, her gaze on him as he put his battered Stetson on his head. She asked in a low tone: "Will they rape her and kill her? Will she be alive when we come home at noon? And if she is, will she be a babbling idiot?"

"We have to believe she'll be all right," he said. "It's the only way we can keep her and Bud alive."

White-faced, Nora nodded, and walked out of the house, her head high. Matt followed her, suddenly proud. *She's going to be all right,* he thought. *This was the front she would show Hannah Talbot and the rest of the women through the morning as they made sandwiches in the Methodist church.*

XVI

Corrigan met Matt and Nora Dugan half a block from their house. He touched the brim of his hat as he nodded at Nora, and said: "Good morning."

They stopped, Nora saying: "Good morning, Jerry." Matt remained silent, but he gave Corrigan a questioning look as if he wanted to say something but couldn't decide whether he should or not.

"Sorry about getting you out of bed last night," Corrigan said. "I'd heard about an outlaw named Ross Hart. It's not a real common name and I started thinking maybe this was the same man, so then I got to worrying about him being in your house."

"He's not the one," Matt said. "I asked Smith about it and he said the outlaw Ross Hart had been killed in a gunfight in Nogales a few days ago."

"I hadn't heard about that," Corrigan said, wondering whether it was true and how Smith happened to know. He thought about saying that Smith struck him as being something he wasn't, then decided not to. If the man really was a cousin, Nora might be insulted and the last thing he wanted to do was to insult his future mother-in-law. "I guess I'll go in and see if Jean can find me a cup of coffee. That is, if she's up."

"Oh, she's up, all right," Nora said. "Well, I've got to run along, Jerry, or Hannah Talbot will be looking for me."

Nora walked past him, moving toward the Methodist church in her usual graceful manner. Corrigan, his gaze following her, thought she could have been a queen. She was a mature woman, yet somehow she managed to give an appearance of youth. Then it struck him that she had been unusually pale.

"Is Nora sick?" Corrigan asked. "She looked a little puny."

Matt hesitated, then he said: "She's just upset. You'd look puny, too, if you had to work with Hannah Talbot all morning."

Corrigan laughed. "I reckon I would at that. Well, I'll go see about that cup of coffee."

"Jerry." Matt threw out a hand to stop him, then hesitated again as if not sure whether he should say what he wanted to say. Finally he blurted: "Damn it, I don't want you to think I'm trying to tell you how to do your job, but I wish you wouldn't stay with Jean very long. I guess I'm a little boogery with this crowd in town and the money for the dam in the bank and all."

Corrigan nodded. "I know what you mean. Uncle Pete Fisher was on my back just a minute ago. He wants to keep the governor out of town, but, hell, I can't do that. I turned the Owl Creek bunch loose and told 'em to get out of town and stay out. They were making some wild threats last night against the governor. Now I dunno. Maybe I should have kept 'em in the jug."

"It's just that I'll feel better knowing you're where the crowd is," Matt said.

"I'll be there," Corrigan promised, and went on past Matt toward the Dugan place.

Corrigan knew that he was jumpy, too,

and he wasn't sure why. He thought about it as he walked through the gate and along the path to the front door. It wasn't Uncle Pete Fisher's warning or the threats the Owl Creek men had made. Maybe, like Matt, it was just having so many people in town for the celebration and having the money in the bank, and knowing, too, that so much depended on the day's going right.

No, he decided, it was more than that. Perhaps it was this business of having a man named Ross Hart in the house, a man he hadn't seen, and then Smith's story that the outlaw had been killed in Nogales. And he couldn't get the haunting notion out of his mind that Smith himself was a phony and Jean was shut up in the house with Ross Hart and a fellow named Sammy Bean who looked like an idiot.

He opened the front door and called: "Jean!" He'd get her out of here, he told himself. He didn't know how, but he'd do it.

"Here, Jerry," Jean answered. "Back in the kitchen."

He went through the house to the kitchen. Bud wasn't in sight, but John Smith was sitting at the table smoking a cigar, and Sammy Bean was across from him wolfing down his breakfast.

"Good morning, Sheriff," Smith said. "Did you get done prowling last night and go to bed?"

"Yeah, I went back to bed," Corrigan answered. "How are you, Bean?"

Sammy Bean looked up from his plate and mumbled something that might have been: "Good morning." His mouth was too full of eggs and bacon to say anything distinctly. He wasn't an idiot. Not at all. His eyes were too sharp and cold and cruel. An animal, perhaps a weasel, but not an idiot.

Bean lowered his gaze again and jammed another bite into his mouth, then rose and hurriedly left the kitchen. He was the kind who instinctively hated law and lawmen. Corrigan wondered if the mere presence of a sheriff in the same room with Bean had been enough to make him uneasy.

Corrigan glanced at Smith who was puffing away on his cigar as if he were perfectly satisfied with life and didn't have a worry in the world. Obviously he wasn't concerned about being in the same room with a sheriff.

Jean set a cup of hot coffee in front of Corrigan. "What's this about being on the prowl?"

"Oh, it wasn't anything," Smith said. "I couldn't sleep last night and I was sitting on the front porch when our young friend showed up and made me get your dad out of bed to answer some silly question about Ross Hart."

Corrigan's temper flared and he opened his mouth, but he closed it before the hot words poured out. To Smith the question might have seemed silly. Besides, maybe Smith really was a cousin, and, if that was true, Corrigan didn't want to quarrel with him for Jean's sake. But Smith did have a way with him, a way of making Corrigan look foolish without saying so.

"If Jerry asked a question in the middle of the night, it wasn't silly," Jean said sharply. "Will you have another cup of coffee?"

"No, thank you, Jean," Smith said. "At the moment my cigar is all the nourishment I need. How are things downtown, Sheriff? Got a big crowd this early in the morning?"

"Not yet," Corrigan said, "but there will be."

"I should think you'd need to circulate around," Smith said in an offhand manner. "You know, just let folks know the law was on the job."

"I'll be there," Corrigan said shortly, wondering what business it was of Smith's whether he was there or here. "Where's Bud, Jean? Looks like he'd be up early on a day like this."

For a moment he sensed that Jean was terrified, her gaze whipping to Smith and back to him as if this question was one she couldn't handle. Smith said: "He's under the weather, Corrigan. Nora said for him to stay in bed until he felt better. You know how it is with kids on the Fourth of July and Christmas and big days like that. They get worked up."

"I've got a headache myself, Jerry," Jean said. "I'm going to stay home."

This was too much. Corrigan said irritably: "You never had a headache in your life."

"I didn't until this morning," Jean said. "Maybe Bud and I are coming down with something. I just don't feel like doing anything."

"She couldn't eat any breakfast," Smith said. "If she hadn't felt she had to wait on us, she probably would have stayed in bed like Bud did."

"I suppose you'll be out buying cattle this morning," Corrigan said.

Smith rose and, going to the stove, tossed his cigar stub into it. "To tell the truth, Sheriff, I'm a little undecided. Like I told you last night, I had hoped to get a loan from Matt's bank, but he's not at all favorable. I couldn't bring myself to come right out and ask him, but I hinted and he sure hinted right back. Maybe we'll have to ride home to Grand Junction without any cattle."

"Why don't you run along, Jerry?" Jean asked. "My head is splitting and I know I'm not good company."

Corrigan rose. Matt and then Smith and now Jean had all suggested that he get back to his business downtown. Bud might be sick in bed, but Corrigan didn't believe for a minute that Jean had a headache.

"All right," Corrigan said, "I'll take a sashay around town. I'll drop in later, Jean. I want to keep tabs on your headache."

"I'll be in bed," she warned.

He nodded at Smith who was fishing in his coat pocket for another cigar. Smith nodded back absently as if his mind was on the loan he wasn't getting from the bank. Corrigan walked into the front room thinking that this might be on the level, that maybe Smith had come here to take advantage of his relationship with Nora to borrow money from the bank. Now it was embarrassing all around.

Sammy Bean was sitting on the couch, a cigarette dangling from the corner of his mouth. He didn't say anything as Corrigan crossed the room to the hall door, but his eyes were pinned on Corrigan all the way to the door.

Suddenly Corrigan had a feeling that sent a chill raveling down his spine. All it would take to start the guns roaring would be a fast, threatening motion on his part. He didn't know why this hunch had come to him unless it was the cold, animal-like stare that Sammy Bean had given him, but the hunch was there and he had learned a long time ago to pay attention when a hunch like this came. If it reached the shooting stage, Jean might be killed. For the moment at least, he had to act as if he didn't suspect anything was wrong.

He left the house, knowing this wasn't on the level at all, but how did you find out what was going on when all you had was a hunch? Sure, it added up with Bud staying in bed on a morning when too much was going on for a boy to miss and Jean having a headache when she had never had a headache in her life as far as he knew and Nora who was usually the picture of health looking as pale as if she were deathly sick.

He paused when he reached the board-walk. Maybe Nora could and would tell him what was going on. At least, he could talk to her without John Smith's hearing every word and Sam Bean's watching him with those cold, weasel eyes of his.

Corrigan turned toward the Methodist church and began to run, sure now that it wasn't just the prospect of working with Hannah Talbot all morning that had made Nora look the way she had.

XVII

Governor Wyatt and Tom Henry ate breakfast by lamplight with Dick Miles in the hotel dining room at Burlington. None felt like talking at this hour. The waitress yawned and rubbed her eyes as she went back to the kitchen with their order.

Wyatt smiled, knowing exactly how the girl felt. He hadn't had a night's sleep for weeks and more weeks would pass before he did. He wondered as he had so many times why he or any man sought a political office only to be criticized and threatened and poorly paid.

Of course, he had better reasons than most politicians had. As a matter of fact he wasn't a politician at all. He was a Populist and that made him a crusader of sorts with new ideas and a new program. This made him suspect to most people who were opposed to new ideas because they were afraid of what the future would bring, so afraid that some of them actually were plotting to murder him.

He sighed as the waitress set his plate of bacon and eggs in front of him. He wasn't hungry, but he ate because he had to keep his strength up for the grueling weeks of the campaign that lay ahead.

He thought about those men in Denver who wanted to see him dead and he was a little surprised at himself for not hating them. Actually he felt sorry for them because they placed such a great value on their wealth, wealth that they were convinced they would lose if he had another term as governor.

Miles bolted his breakfast and rose. "I'll fetch the team and rig to the front door, Governor," he said. "It won't be more than ten minutes."

"We'll be there," Wyatt promised.

Miles swung around and strode out of the dining room. Henry stared at his back, frowning. "I don't trust that man. I still think we should send word to Amity that you can't make it and catch the next train out of here."

Wyatt sighed and, picking up his cup, drank the rest of his coffee. He said: "You're still thinking about that death threat, Tom. I won't disappoint the people in Amity because we get a letter from another crackpot."

"I don't think it was a crackpot this time," Henry said. "We've known for a month or more that there was a conspiracy in Denver. . . ."

"I know, I know," Wyatt said testily as he rose. "Let me remind you that there is a good deal of difference between a conspiracy and an actual effort to kill me. Now let's go get our luggage and be ready when Miles gets here with his rig."

Henry's jaw jutted forward stubbornly. "It's a waste of time and effort. You won't get a vote from that bunch down there. You ought to save your strength. . . ."

"Tom, sometimes you try me severely," Wyatt said. "There are a few worthwhile things in this campaign besides getting votes. Now, come on."

From long experience, Tom Henry knew how far he could go with Wyatt and he had reached that point. He followed Wyatt out of the dining room and up the stairs to their room. A few minutes later Wyatt closed and locked his suitcase and set it in the hall outside his door. Henry picked it up and carried it and his own bag downstairs and put them down on the boardwalk in front of the hotel.

A moment later Wyatt joined him just as Miles drew up in a hack. Henry piled the suitcases in the back and stepped up and sat down beside Wyatt in the rear seat.

Miles handed two rifles to Wyatt and Henry, asking: "How are you gents on the shoot?"

"I'm pretty good," Wyatt said as he took the Winchester. "Are we stopping to hunt jack rabbits?"

Miles scowled. "You know damned well why I'm handing out these Thirty-Thirties. We may go clean through to Amity without any trouble, but again maybe we won't. I figure three rifles is a hell of a lot better than one. If we get stopped, show that we're armed and do it fast."

Henry had taken his rifle and carefully placed it between him and Wyatt as Miles turned and spoke to the team. Wyatt couldn't keep from grinning as he winked at Henry. He said: "Well, Tom, are you ready to defend yourself?"

"I told you we shouldn't make this trip," Henry said. "It ain't worth it to risk our necks just to give a talk about a dam."

Wyatt guessed that Henry had never fired a rifle in his life, but he didn't lack courage. That fact had been demonstrated more than once in the time they had been associated. He said gently: "That's a matter of opinion. You may be proved right, but in my opinion it is worth risking our necks for and my opinion is the one we have to go by."

Henry's face turned red. "Yes, sir," he said. "I know that. It's just that I hate to take the risk of having you assassinated."

"We take that risk every time I make a speech," Wyatt said.

They were silent then, the town dropping behind. The road led straight south through a rolling land covered by grass and sagebrush and Spanish bayonet. The dust rose behind them in a gray cloud and hung there in the still morning air while the sun moved up into a blue sky.

It was warm now, but Wyatt knew that by noon, when they were due to reach Amity, the temperature would be in the nineties. He would have to stand on a platform under that hot sun to make a speech, and then he would get back into a rig and ride north to Burlington to catch a westbound train.

It was too much, he told himself. Just too damned much, but he had made a commitment and he would keep it if it killed him. It might do exactly that, too. He had felt the heat more this summer than ever before. A day like this could give him a heart attack or heat prostration or something of the sort. Tom Henry had apparently not thought of it, but Wyatt considered it a greater danger than an assassin's bullet.

The country was monotonously the same, with here and there the buildings of a cattle ranch set back from the road. Wyatt didn't like eastern Colorado. He had spent much of his life before becoming governor in the mining camps high in the Rockies. He loved the scenery which was never quite the same, the invigorating air of the high country, the variety of colors, the pale green of the quaking aspens or their gold in the fall, the dark green of the pines, the sharp green of the grass in the mountain meadows.

If he lost the election, he would go back to the high country. There were times, and this was one, when he actually hoped he did lose. Then quite suddenly he dropped off to sleep, his chin dipping to his chest, his head bobbing back and forth. An hour later he woke suddenly as Miles yanked the team to a stop, cursing furiously.

"Here they come, Governor," Miles said. "Let 'em see your Winchesters. Both of 'em."

It took Wyatt a moment before he could fully comprehend what was happening. Tom Henry had lined his rifle on three cowboys who were riding toward them. Miles wrapped the lines around the brake handle, then picked up his Winchester. Wyatt rubbed his eyes and moistened his dry lips with the tip of his tongue, then lifted his rifle across his lap so it could be seen.

"Who are they?" he asked.

"In town we call 'em the Owl Creek boys," Miles answered. "They've got shirt-tail spreads up Owl Creek and they make a hell of a poor living on 'em. They're like a lot of cowmen around Amity. They blame you and the Populist party 'cause they're almost broke."

"How do you know they're after me?"

"I've heard 'em talk." Miles motioned at the three riders and called: "That's close enough! I'm taking the governor to town to speak at noon. We haven't got time to stop and palaver, so if you've got anything to say, spit it out and get to hell off the road."

The three men pulled up and sat their saddles, their eyes on Miles as if surprised to run into him. One of them started to curse as he reached for his gun, then froze as Miles cocked his rifle.

"Don't do it, Yarnell," Miles said. "I figured some of you tough hands might try something like this, so we fetched along three Winchesters. Just start the ball, boys, and we'll finish it."

"What is it?" Wyatt asked. "Are you men here to see me?"

"We're here to kill you," the one Miles had called Yarnell said, "but we didn't figger to run into three rifles. Maybe you and your friend can't hit anything, but that damned Miles can shoot a fly off a man's nose at fifty yards. What's the matter with you, Dick?"

"That's what I'd like to know," another one said truculently. "You're a cowboy and you know what that old goat has done to us. We just sold all the steers we could round up and we got about enough *dinero* for 'em to pay taxes. What the hell are we supposed to live on?"

"Get off the road or you won't need to worry about having anything to live on," Miles said. "You don't have to like the governor, but you're going to treat him real polite. You hear me, Lupton?"

Wyatt laughed. "I've been called worse names than an old goat," he said. "Gentlemen, I'm sorry about the low price of beef, but I don't know why you blame me. If you've got to blame somebody, blame the bankers. As governor, my program has been stopped in the legislature by the bankers and other wealthy men in the state."

"Oh, hell," Yarnell said. "Don't cuss the bankers. If there's one decent man in Amity, the banker's him, but you probably never heard of Matt Dugan."

"On the contrary," Wyatt said, "he's the one who asked me to come to Amity to speak today. He'll be disappointed if you kill me."

"You're drunk," Miles said. "No sense trying to talk to you. Get out of our way."

"Sure we're drunk," Yarnell said. "Everybody will be drunk before Dam Day's over." He scratched a stubble-covered cheek as he stared at Wyatt. "We didn't know you were here to speak because Matt invited you."

"Yeah, we sure didn't," Lupton agreed. "Maybe we won't kill you, after all."

Miles laughed at them. "Of course you won't. You're a pack of fools. If you start anything . . . anything at all, I'll see all three of you hang just as sure as you're the ugliest man on Owl Creek."

Miles put his rifle down and, taking the lines, spoke to the team and drove straight at Yarnell and Lupton. Grudgingly they reined to one side of the road and the rig wheeled past them.

"Watch behind you," Miles said. "I bluffed 'em that time and I don't look for trouble now, but they've been drinking, and sometimes whiskey gives men like that enough guts to do what they wouldn't do any other time."

Wyatt and Henry turned to watch the three cowboys who were holding their horses in the road as if not sure what they should do now. Wyatt said: "They're not chasing us."

"This is about what I expected," Miles said. "We'll still keep our eyes peeled. I figure them three are mostly blow, but there's men in Amity who ain't."

Wyatt glanced at Henry. He said: "No, we're not going back to Burlington even after that."

He didn't sleep any more. For the first time he came to grips with the hard fact that Tom Henry had been right about the danger they would be facing in Amity. He had been underestimating it in his own thinking. The men he had just seen had suffered enough and had been drunk enough to have killed him if Dick Miles had not handled them exactly the way he had.

There would be other men in Amity waiting to see him, men who had suffered as much and would be as drunk as these three. He was heading into a hornets' nest. It was his business if he chose to face danger, but he had no right to take Tom Henry with him.

He turned to look at Henry's set face, wanting to ask him to get out of the rig before they reached Amity. He turned his head again to stare at the long, gray ribbon of road ahead of them. He couldn't do it. Henry would be insulted if he did.

XVIII

Bud Dugan slept fitfully and woke several times during the night. Dolly was always awake, sometimes walking around the room, and sometimes sitting in the rawhide-bottom chair at the table, playing solitaire. When it was daylight, he woke again in time to see Dolly coming toward him, two rawhide thongs in her hand.

When she saw that he was awake, she said: "I'm gonna tie you up. I'm so damned sleepy I'm about to fall on my face. I've got to go to bed for a while, and I can't trust you to stay put."

She tied his feet first, then tied his hands behind his back. She took the shell out of the shotgun and left the gun lying across the table. Now she walked past the table to one of the shelves in the corner and returned with a revolver.

"You go on back to sleep," she said. "I'm gonna lie right there beside you. I sleep light, so if you get loose, which I don't figure you will, and if you try to go outside, I'll plug you right in the brisket."

She sprawled out on the bed beside him, the revolver clutched in her right hand, and was asleep in a matter of seconds. He turned his head to look at her. She snored with gusto; her lips fluttered with each outgoing breath. Sometimes she would choke and snort and wake herself up, and then she would go back to sleep at once.

If circumstances had been different, he would have laughed. Dolly looked and sounded comical enough, but he couldn't laugh. He thought there was a good chance he would never laugh again as long as he lived.

The woman was an animal. She'd kill him if he tried to get away just as she had said she would. He lay on his side, thinking of his mother and then Jean and finally of his father. Up until now Matt Dugan had been the kind of man who could do anything.

Bud found it hard to believe that for the first time in his life Matt was caught in a trap that made it impossible for him to do anything. But he hadn't panicked. Bud was thankful for that. A lesser man than his father would have cracked under the pressure and either made a run for it himself or helped Bud get out through a window and go after Jerry Corrigan.

At that first moment when his father had awakened him, Bud had thought he should go for help, but now, with time to think about it, he knew his father had been right. They were dealing with people who had no conscience, who were here to murder someone for a large amount of money.

He watched the light deepen in the soddy as the sun rose. Dolly had not been an expert at tying his wrists. The thong was not tight, and now he began to twist his hands back and forth and to tighten and relax his muscles. He found after a few minutes of this that he had increased the slack.

Still, it was a long time before he was able to slip his hands through the loop. When he did succeed in freeing himself, he brought his hands around in front of him and gently massaged his wrists. They were raw, a good deal of the skin having been rubbed off, but he was free. He sat up, moving slowly and carefully so he wouldn't wake Dolly, and untied the thong around his ankles.

All this time he had been carefully weighing his chances of getting out of the soddy alive. He still didn't know what Jerry Corrigan could do if he were told what was going on, but the situation was different than it had been last night. If he had left the house then, Smith and the other two would soon have known and there would have been hell to pay. Now, if he escaped from the soddy, Dolly wouldn't ride into town to tell Smith and Sammy what had happened. If she rode anywhere, she'd ride the other way.

He looked at the woman. She had moved so she lay partly on her side. He had hoped he could get the revolver away from her, but she had rolled over enough so that the gun was partly under her. He couldn't possibly pull it free without waking her, and the shotgun wouldn't do him any good if he was able to get to it. He didn't know what she had done with the shell.

All he could do was to slip off the bed and cat-foot to the door, lift the bar and open the door, and then light out for the shed as fast as he could run. If he made it that far, the chances were good he could saddle his horse and ride to town.

Bud was perfectly aware that he might never reach the door. Or reaching it, he might wake her when he lifted the bar. The door might squeak when he opened it. She'd shoot him like a dog if she woke up before he got away.

He was scared. He had never been as scared in his whole life as he was right now. When he looked at her face, he felt prickles run up and down his spine; he felt his belly muscles contract until they were hugging his backbone. Scared or not, he knew he had to try to get out.

The thought came to him that this was his initiation into manhood. If he made it, he'd be a man. If he didn't, he'd be dead, but he was certain that, if his father were in his position and felt there was a chance to get Jean and her mother out of danger, he'd do anything he could to save them. Or Jerry Corrigan. They were the best men he knew, and he could do no less than they would under the same circumstances.

Carefully he eased off the bed and stood up, his eyes on Dolly. She didn't move or miss a snore. His heart began to pound as he moved silently across the room, the longest fifteen feet he had ever covered in his life. He got to the door and looked back. She still hadn't moved.

He turned his head and lifted the bar, thinking he had made it, but just as he eased the bar to the floor and reached for the knob to open the door, Dolly's revolver roared, a bullet slapped into the door within an inch of the side of his head, and she bellowed: "Put the bar back, damn it! What'd I tell you I'd do if you tried to leave?"

For a few seconds he couldn't move. He

expected her to shoot again and the next time she wouldn't miss. When the bullet didn't come, he reached for the bar, replaced it, and slowly turned.

"I wasn't trying to get away," he said. "It's getting stuffy in here. Besides, I needed some exercise. You had me tied so tight the circulation was stopped and I figured I was getting gangrene."

"You're a damned liar." She got up, the revolver in her hand. "I'll say one thing for you, boy. You're the coolest customer I ever ran into." She motioned to the bed. "Get back over here."

He obeyed. She crossed the room, lifted the bar, and opened the door. She stood in the sunlight and took a deep breath, then turned to face him. "You're right about one thing. It was getting purty stuffy. Staying in one of these damn' soddies is like living in a cave."

"I'm hungry," he said. "Is part of your job to starve me to death?"

She scratched her head, then shrugged. "No it ain't. A cup of coffee would go purty good."

She laid the revolver on the table and built a fire. He had a wild hope that she might move far enough from the table so he'd have a chance at the gun. He had no illusions about what she'd do if he tried for it and failed, but he'd try if he thought the odds of his getting his hands on it ahead of hers were about equal.

The chance never came. She put the coffee pot on the stove, fished some bacon sandwiches out of a greasy sack, and gave him one. When the coffee was done, she filled two tin cups and handed one to him, then stepped back to the table. At no time was she more than ten feet from the revolver.

There was another way of getting at her. He remembered that she had told Sammy last night that she wasn't staying here for a posse to find. She looked as mean as ever, but she hadn't killed him as she said she would if he tried to get away. She was softer than she let on.

He said in an offhand tone: "If they've got the murdering done, I'll bet those three men are out of the country by now and a posse will be showing up here any time."

She was drinking coffee when he said that. She gulped and choked and fought for breath for a good part of a minute. When she was able to talk, she said: "You shut up. You're a purty foxy kid, but it ain't gonna work."

"I was thinking that they don't just arrest

246

the ones who do the killing," he said. "I mean the ones who do the shooting. They arrest everybody who had anything to do with the murder. They hang all of 'em. Did you ever see anybody hang?"

She glared at him, her big fists doubled, then she whirled to the table and picked up the revolver. "I didn't kill you a while ago when I had plenty of reason to," she said, "but I ain't gonna go easy again. You'd better shut your big, flappin' mouth."

For the time being that was all he could do. He had goaded her as much as he could for now, but he'd given her something to think about. She laid the gun down and reached for her coffee cup, her hand trembling so much that she spilled several drops.

He thought: *Sooner or later she's going to break and I'll get out of here.* But he knew it might not be in time.

XIX

The Methodist church was buzzing with activity when Jerry Corrigan arrived. A dozen or more women were making sandwiches, working at tables that had been set up in the slim shadow of the building. In another hour or so the sun would be blasting at them, the shade completely gone.

Hannah Talbot was having the time of her life. She had her hand on the throttle, running in and out of the church or moving from one woman to another to find fault with the work that woman was doing. When a tray of sandwiches was finished, she would send Parson Hess trotting toward the courthouse with it, admonishing him to be sure the sandwiches were covered with a tablecloth because the flies were just terrible.

If the preacher wasn't on hand, Mrs. Talbot sent one of the women with the sandwiches, but Corrigan noticed that she didn't send Nora Dugan to the courthouse and she was never critical of the way Nora cut the bread or spread the butter or of the amount of ham or chicken she placed between the slices.

Nora was not aware of his presence until he moved up to stand beside her and asked: "How's it going?"

Startled, she glanced up. Tiny beads of perspiration made her face glisten. She wiped her face with a wadded-up handkerchief, then said: "All right, Jerry. Hannah's worried about not having enough sandwiches, and I guess there are an awful lot of people in town."

"Yeah, there sure are," he agreed.

He didn't see Hannah Talbot come up

until she said: "I didn't expect to see you around here today, Sheriff. I thought you'd be out lollygagging' with Jean."

He scowled, thinking there wasn't anyone else in the whole world he disliked as heartily as he did Hannah Talbot. He said: "I wish I was."

She smirked as if to tell him she knew he couldn't hit her as he would have a man, then she said with a nasty curl of her lips: "I think you two had better get married before it's too late."

She walked off, switching her behind at him. He clenched his fists and stared after her, then he said: "So help me, someday I'll forget she's a woman." He glanced at Nora. She was still pale, but she seemed to feel all right. "How do you keep that old heifer off your back?"

"I don't know," Nora said, "but I am the only woman here she hasn't clawed a few times this morning." She moistened her lips, glancing at Corrigan, and then turned her gaze back to the loaf of bread she was slicing. "How was Jean when you left the house?"

"I think she was fine," Corrigan answered, "but she claims Bud's sick in bed and she's got a headache and she's going back to bed and she didn't feel like coming with me. I don't believe any of it, Nora."

For a time Nora said nothing. All Corrigan could hear was the chatter of the women and Parson Hess's heavy voice and the scream of children playing behind the church. Finally Nora said: "You aren't accusing Jean of lying to you, are you, Jerry?"

"I don't like to put it that way," he admitted, "but I've got a hunch that something's wrong. By this time, it's more'n a hunch. I don't like the idea of Jean being in the house with those three men even if two of 'em are supposed to be her cousins."

She continued slicing bread, and Corrigan, his gaze dropping to her hands, noticed that they were trembling. She was slicing the bread too thick and he wondered if Hannah Talbot would tell her so.

"Jean will be all right," Nora said finally. "If you're worried, why don't you talk to Matt about it?"

He wondered if she were trying to tell him something without coming out and saying it directly. He had always found her a direct and forthright woman, but now he was convinced she was holding back facts she should tell him.

"You're saying that something's wrong but you'd rather have Matt tell me," he said. "Is that it?" She didn't answer, but he saw that the corners of her mouth were quivering. "Who are those men?" he demanded. "Are they really cousins?"

"Talk to Matt," she said in a tone so low he hardly heard her above the racket around them. "If he wants to tell you, all right. I can't, Jerry. I just can't."

He saw Hannah Talbot coming toward them under full sail. He didn't want to be there if Mrs. Talbot was going to chew Nora out for making the slices of bread too thick, so he said: "All right, I will." He wheeled and strode away.

The crowd was beginning to assemble in front of the courthouse. The job of putting up the bunting on the platform was finished, and, although it was too early for the band to gather, several members were sitting on the chairs that had been placed at the end of the platform for them. They were resplendent in their bright red uniforms with the gold buttons, and some were making strange, discordant noises on their trombones and coronets.

Corrigan hurried past them, toward the business block, refusing to be delayed by a fight that was brewing between two cowboys. As far as he was concerned, they could go ahead and kill each other if that was what they wanted to do. He wasn't sure that Matt would tell him any more than Nora had, but he was going to put it up to him anyhow.

The main part of the crowd was here on Main Street, the women seeking any shade they could find and most of the men moving in and out of the saloons. Corrigan strode toward the bank as fast as he could, shouldering through the crowd, sometimes not very politely because he was goaded by a sense of urgency. He wanted Jean out of the Dugan house, and, if Matt didn't get her out, he'd do it himself.

When he stepped into the bank, he saw that a dozen men were lined up in front of the teller's cage. Fred Follett was waiting on them, but Matt was not in sight. There was a second teller's cage where Matt usually worked when there was a crowd, but he wasn't in it today. The door to his private office in the back was closed. Corrigan hesitated only a moment, glancing at Follett, then he shoved the gate back at the end of the counter and went on toward Matt's office.

Follett saw him and called: "Wait, Sheriff! I'll tell Mister Dugan you want to see him. Unless it's a matter of grave importance, I don't think. . . ."

"You're busy," Corrigan said curtly. "Stay where you are. This is official business."

He opened the door without knocking, stepped into the room, and closed the door. Matt sat at his desk, his head in his hands. He said without looking up: "What is it, Fred?"

"I'm not Fred." Corrigan pulled up a chair and sat down. "What's going on, Matt?"

"Nothing." Matt rubbed his face with both hands and looked at Corrigan. "The big question is what's going on out there in the street? Probably about ten fights. Why aren't you keeping the peace instead of coming in here?"

"What's going on?" Corrigan asked again, irritated by Matt's effort to divert him.

"Why, it's Dam Day," Matt said heavily. "I don't know why I have to tell you what's going on."

Anger replaced irritation in Corrigan. He leaned forward. "Matt, I want to know what's going on in your house. Now you'd better quit acting so damned innocent."

"Did you see Jean?"

"Yes, I saw Jean. I've just come from the church where I talked to Nora. She wouldn't tell me anything, but she said for me to talk to you. Now you'd better tell me what's happening."

"Jean didn't do very well, I guess. I told

her she'd have to do a good job of acting." Matt looked past Corrigan at the opposite wall, refusing to meet his eyes. "Is Smith still there? I thought he might come downtown."

"All right, Matt." Corrigan leaned forward. "I had a kind of a hunch last night when I looked Ross Hart up and got you out of bed. I should have hauled Smith off to jail, but I didn't have enough to go on. Now I do, and I'm as sure as I'm sitting here that something's wrong. Real wrong. I don't believe those two so-called cattle buyers are Nora's cousins at all. I don't think they're even cattle buyers."

"I never heard Nora speak of them before," Matt admitted uneasily, "but. . . ."

Corrigan rose. "I'm done talking, Matt. I'm going to your house and I'm going to haul Jean out of there. It may be too late now, but I can't stand it any longer."

"Sit down." Matt motioned to the chair. "I'll tell you, but you've got to go along with me. Until I'm ready to make a move, you've got to stay out of it. Agreed?"

Corrigan hesitated. Matt Dugan was a man whose judgment he had always valued, but he was under some kind of pressure now and his judgment might be wrong. Still, it seemed to Corrigan, he had to trust

Matt; he had to believe that no amount of pressure would change his basically sound judgment.

Corrigan sat down. "All right, Matt."

Leaning back in his chair, Matt took a long breath, his gaze on Corrigan. "Jerry, I'm warning you not to go off half cocked. I've had to live with this ever since I went home from the meeting last night and I don't know yet how to handle it. You're right. Those men are not Nora's cousins and they are not cattle buyers."

Matt took another breath and, leaning forward now, put his hands palm down on his desk. "Jerry, they're bank robbers. They have Jean as a hostage in the house and Bud somewhere out in the country. They have promised that if we co-operate, neither Jean nor Bud will be hurt. At noon when the governor arrives and there's a lot of excitement, I'm to take ten thousand dollars home and these men will get out of town and release Jean and Bud."

Corrigan sat motionlessly, barely breathing. He could think only of Jean, held there in the house with three outlaws. He had no trust in them, no belief whatever that they would keep their word. By this time she might have been attacked by any or all of them, or killed, or both.

"I've been over this in my mind a hundred times," Matt went on. "If we were lucky and went into the house and shot it out with them, we might clean them out and save Jean, but it wouldn't save Bud. I don't know where they're keeping him, but they've got him and I can't take a chance on them killing him if I don't do what they say."

"What are you going to do?" Corrigan asked hoarsely.

"The only thing I can do," Matt said. "I'll deliver the money and trust them to keep their word. Later, we'll get a posse together and go after them, but not until Jean and Bud are safe."

Corrigan took a long breath. Matt was right. They couldn't sacrifice Bud's life. Maybe they couldn't trust these men to keep their word, but the hard fact was they had Jean and they had Bud. A crazy wildness began working through Corrigan. He wanted to go to the house and kill all three of them. When he thought about his future without Jean, he could see no reason to live.

Matt was watching him anxiously. "You won't do anything to pressure them, will you, Jerry? Ten thousand dollars is cheap enough for their lives."

Corrigan rose and stood looking down at Matt. "Suppose they take Jean with them

256

for a hostage when they leave? We can't go after them if they do."

"No," Matt said, "we can't."

Jerry Corrigan turned to the door and opened it and stumbled out of the office. He crossed to the street door and went out into the crowd. He blindly pushed people aside as he walked toward the courthouse, all the time asking himself why this had happened.

You fall in love and you make plans for the future and you can see nothing but happiness ahead of you, then everything is snatched away and destroyed. Why? Why? Why? There was no answer. Only the question, and an impossible situation about which he could do nothing.

XX

Matt remained at his desk after Corrigan left the bank. He could do nothing except wait until it was time to take the $10,000 to the house. He had already moved it from the safe to his office. After the outlaws were gone and Jean was safe, and after a little more time had passed so Bud would be released, Matt would help Jerry Corrigan gather a posse and they would go after the outlaws.

But now the minutes dragged. He closed his eyes and leaned back in his chair, and found that he couldn't relax. The pounding of his heart seemed to jar his whole body. His head ached, too. It was the waiting, he thought, more than the blow he had received on his head that caused it, the waiting and the uncertainty about Jean and Bud. If the outlaws did not keep their word, and if his children were killed, he would blame himself the rest of his life for not bringing the whole thing to a head.

Suddenly he was aware that someone was arguing with Fred Follett outside his office. He rose and opened the door. Uncle Pete Fisher was trying to get into his office to see him, and Follett was trying to keep him out.

When Fisher saw him, he bawled: "Get this pup off my neck, Matt! I've got to talk to you."

"He's drunk," Follett said in disgust. "He's drunk as a lord. Jerry ought to lock him up. I don't know of anything that's worse than an old man who's drunk."

"Let him come in," Matt said.

Follett threw up his hands and wheeled back into his cage. The men who were waiting in front of the cage laughed. One of them said: "Nothing's worse than an old

258

has-been, is there, Fred?"

"Unless it's a drunk one," Follett said angrily. "Matt should have had me throw the old fool out."

Matt shut the door, thinking that Follett might be right. Uncle Pete had been a problem for quite a while and he would probably get worse as he grew older. Matt noticed that his beard and mustache were white, he was filthy, and he stunk with the second-hand smell of cheap whiskey. Matt felt his stomach begin to churn, but he sat down, thinking Fisher wouldn't be here long.

"What's wrong, Uncle Pete?" Matt asked.

Fisher sat in the chair Corrigan had occupied a short time before, his head tipped forward, his gaze on the floor. Suddenly he began to cry, sobs shaking his gnarled old body.

For a time Fisher couldn't answer Matt's question. Matt, as disgusted as Follett had been, decided he'd throw the old man out himself, then Fisher swiped a dirty sleeve across his eyes. He looked up and swallowed, he opened his mouth to say something and closed it and swallowed.

Finally Fisher was able to talk. He said: "Matt, do you know what it's like to be a big man in a community like this, and then drop to nothing?" Fisher wiped his face with both hands, then he went on: "I've sat right there at the same desk and in that same chair you're sitting in, and I've said to men who were in this chair that I'd save their hides by giving 'em the loan they were asking for, or I'd say they couldn't have it even if I knew I was going to break 'em. I was playing God, Matt. You savvy that?"

Matt frowned. The old man was drunk, all right, but something had made him get drunk because he usually limited himself to two drinks a day. Matt thought: *Whatever made him keep drinking brought him here. I'd better keep him talking and find out what it is.* "I savvy," Matt said. "Go on."

"I'm still playing God," Fisher went on. "Now you've got to help me 'cause it's more'n I can handle. I hate the governor and the Populists. It was Benjamin Wyatt who took me out of that chair where you're sitting. I hate him and I want to see him dead, but I just never knew how it was going to be, having him killed here in Amity on Dam Day."

Matt froze. He stared at Fisher, unable to believe what he had heard, but the agony of hell that was twisting the old man's face told him he'd better believe it.

"Go on," Matt said. "Tell me all about it."

260

"I'm fixing to," Fisher said. "It's been eating on me and I kept drinking till now I guess I've got myself drunk enough to tell you. I'm ashamed, Matt. I'm ashamed because I didn't think that killing Ben Wyatt here in Amity on a day like this would ruin the land sale and give us a black eye all over the state. I don't want my friends hurt, you and everybody else that's worked hard on this whole business and put everything you had into it." Fisher stopped.

Matt said: "Go on, Pete. Tell me exactly what's going to happen."

"There's some men in Denver who want Wyatt killed," Fisher said, staring at the floor. "Rich men. They want him out of the way so bad they'll pay for getting him killed. They know that, if he stays governor, and it kind 'o looks like he'll get re-elected, Colorado will go broke and everybody's gonna lose anything they've got left. The only way to save the state and for these men to save what they've got is to see that Wyatt is rubbed out. I sent 'em information about you and your family and your house. They picked three men to come here and move into your place and shoot Wyatt when he gets up to talk. All I done is to tell 'em how it was here. The Denver men did everything else."

261

Fisher's Adam's apple bobbed up and down as he struggled to swallow again. He went on: "The three men are supposed to tell you they're here to rob the bank, but that's just an excuse they're gonna give you. We figured you'd stand still for that if it was a proposition of saving the lives of your kids, but you wouldn't stand still for murdering the governor. I know they're in your house 'cause I looked in your barn this morning and I seen three strange horses. I ain't seen Bud around the courthouse and he was supposed to help Cole with the tables. I ain't seen Jean, neither, and she's not one to stay home on a day like this. And Nora, she looks like a walking corpse."

He began to cry again, but he managed to blubber: "I hated Wyatt so much I didn't see how it would work out. All I could think of was getting even with him. Now you gotta stop him. You gotta keep Dick Miles from coming into town with him."

Matt got to his feet, so furious with Fisher he wanted to reach out and grab him by the throat and strangle him. He had heard Fisher ramble on about how much he hated Wyatt and the Populists, and how everybody would be ruined if Wyatt was reëlected governor, but he had never even dreamed the old man was actually capable of doing anything that would harm Wyatt. Now Matt, thinking of the three men in his house, could and did believe everything that Fisher had said.

"You fool!" Matt said. "You old fool! Do you know what can happen to Jean and Bud because of your infernal scheming?"

Fisher didn't answer. He was crying softly now, his head bobbing back and forth as the tears poured down his cheeks and ran into his mustache and beard.

"There's a hundred houses in this town," Matt raged. "Why did you have to pick mine?"

"It had the best location," Fisher mumbled. "Your upstairs window in Nora's sewing room looks right at the platform where Wyatt is to stand. Stop him, Matt. You got to stop him."

"And I've got a girl and a boy they can use for hostages," Matt said in a low tone. "They can kill them to save their hides if it comes to that. I ought to beat you to death, Pete. I ought to drag you out of that chair and break your worthless neck."

"I didn't think," Fisher moaned. "I got to talking to them rich men in Denver and I was tellin 'em about Wyatt coming here and how easy it would be to shoot him from your upstairs window and the first thing I knew they had it all worked out. I hate Wyatt 'cause he ruined me. I've got to beg my wife for money to even buy a drink. Beg her on my hands and knees because I'm broke. I didn't think about Jean and Bud getting hurt. Or about the dam, either."

"My God, you didn't think." Matt wheeled to the door, knowing he had to find Corrigan and there was so little time. "You stay right there. Jerry will take care of you. Don't try to get away."

Matt ran out of his office and past Fred Follett and the men lined in front of the teller's cage. He raced on out of the bank and into the street and pushed and jammed his way through the crowd. He had no idea where to find Corrigan. Probably around the courthouse.

He asked several men if they had seen Corrigan. None had. Matt worked clear of the crowd and ran along the street toward the courthouse. Then he saw Corrigan in front of the platform talking to Cole Talbot. Most of the band was here now, producing noise but no music.

Matt yelled: "Jerry!" Again he started jamming his way through the crowd. He yelled — "Jerry!" — a second time, but there was still too much racket for him to be heard. When he reached Corrigan, he grabbed his arm, saying: "I've got to see you, Jerry."

Irritated, Corrigan wheeled away from Talbot, saw who it was, and nodded. He turned back to Talbot. "I'll help you later if you need it, Cole."

Using their shoulders and elbows to get through the crowd, they forced their way to the street. Matt told Corrigan what Fisher had said, and added: "We'll go ahead as planned. I'll take the money at noon, but you've got to saddle up and ride out to meet Dick Miles. I don't care what you tell them, but keep them from coming into town. As far as anybody else goes, we'll keep mum about the assassination scheme."

Corrigan's pulse was pounding in his temples. He said: "Matt, Wyatt won't be easy to stop. He may give us a little extra time, but I don't figure he'll stay out of town all afternoon while we figure out what to do."

"I'm sure he won't," Matt said. "He's a stubborn old man and he's got more'n his share of guts. Make him give us half an hour. I'll have a gun when I go into the house. You be in the barn. I'll start the ball if I get an opening, and you can give me a hand from the back. I don't know how it'll work out, so we'll have to play our cards the way they fall, but we can't just sit tight.

We've got to get at 'em some way, and I can get into the house with the money without making a fuss."

Corrigan didn't like it and showed it in his face. He said: "They'll kill you, Matt."

"Then I'll be dead," Matt said irritably. "It's a price I'm willing to pay to save Jean. The governor, too, but I don't know about Bud. I wish to hell I did, but we haven't got time to find out about him."

"All right," Corrigan said, and wheeled and ran toward the livery stable.

Matt returned to the bank, walking slowly. He felt whipped, and he had little faith that his plan would do any good, but there seemed to be nothing else he could do. Fisher had been right about his standing still for a bank robbery, but he couldn't stand still for the governor to be murdered.

He went into the bank and walked on back to his office, then he saw that Uncle Pete Fisher was gone.

XXI

I wait, Bud Dugan told himself over and over. *I've got to wait till that she-devil quits and runs for it.*

She would, he knew. He watched her pace back and forth in the soddy, go to the door and look down the slope toward Amity, then turn and pace some more. All the time her face and neck grew redder and redder, her breathing louder and louder until she was practically panting.

She'll blow up pretty soon, Bud thought. *She'll scream like a stepped-on cat and go running out of here to the shed. She'll saddle up and hightail out of the country.*

Still she stayed. He sat on the bed and watched every move she made, and all the time he was thinking of his mother and Jean in the house with three killers. He knew his mother was scheduled to help Hannah Talbot with the sandwiches. If she told the outlaws, they'd probably let her go and tell her to keep her mouth shut, but the chances were they'd keep Jean in the house and he couldn't bear to think what they might do to her during the morning.

In spite of all he could do, tears ran down his cheeks. He was remembering that he was supposed to help Cole Talbot with the tables. Cole was kind of a mean man, and he'd be sore because Bud hadn't showed up. He'd go to the bank and ask where Bud was. Bud wondered what his dad would say.

Hard to tell what Jerry Corrigan would do, too. He was no fool. If he caught on to what was happening, and Bud figured he would, he might let his temper go and sail into the house with his gun in his hand and start shooting. He'd get killed, and then Jean would be killed.

Bud wiped a sleeve across his eyes. Here he was, sitting on the bed in Uncle Pete Fisher's soddy. He could put a stop to the whole business if he could get away. No, he couldn't stop the whole business, but he could tell Jerry, and Jerry would know what to do if he thought about it. He guessed Jerry would know what to do about anything as long as his temper didn't make him go off half cocked.

He wiped his sweaty face, his gaze never leaving Dolly as she prowled around the room like an oversize cat. Several times he tensed his muscles to jump her if she came close enough to him, then he always relaxed, reminding himself that it would be certain suicide. He wouldn't free Jean by getting himself killed.

But time was running out. From inside the soddy he couldn't see the sun, but it had to be close to noon. Whatever was going to happen would be happening before very many more minutes passed. He couldn't wait any longer.

"Uncle Pete Fisher used to tell us kids about the lynchings he had seen in Denver,"

Bud said, his voice high-pitched and excited. "He said their necks got real long as their bodies fell. . . ."

"Kid, I told you to shut your big mouth." Dolly wheeled on him, her big fists clenched, her face going ugly from the fury that swept over her. "You keep that up and I'll bust you a good one."

"And their faces turned purple," he went on. "He said their tongues were sticking out of their mouths something awful. He told us it made him throw up, it was so horrible. I got to thinking about you. . . ."

She rushed toward him and hit him on the side of the head, a powerful blow that knocked him flat on his back across the bed. She grabbed up the thongs she had used to tie him early that morning and yanked both hands in front of him. She tied his wrists, then lashed the other thong around his ankles. She was trembling, her face so red it was almost purple.

"I'm going to the shed and saddle my horse, so I'll be ready to get out of here as soon as they come!" she yelled as she picked up the shotgun and revolver from the table. "Maybe you'll get loose again, but you'd better stay right here if you do. I'll blow your damned head off if you don't."

She ran out of the soddy. He told himself

she was bluffing. She wasn't staying here waiting for the men to come, but knowing that didn't help much. He strained at the thong that bound his wrists, but he couldn't get enough slack to free his hands.

Time, he kept telling himself. He didn't have time to lie here all day, but he couldn't untie the knot with his teeth. He tried. He just couldn't get a solid bite on the thong to pull the knot loose, then he realized that the rawhide was stretching, that he had more slack than he'd had a moment before.

Within two or three minutes his hands were free. It took only a few more seconds to untie his ankles. He ran to the door, thinking he would get his horse and light out for town, then he stopped. Maybe the woman was out there at the shed. He hadn't heard her ride away, but it didn't prove anything because he'd been so intent on getting free that he probably wouldn't have heard a company of cavalry ride past.

He slipped along the front of the sod house, reached the corner, and peered around it, showing as little of himself as possible. Dolly wasn't in sight. Neither were the horses. She had taken his horse, too.

Dolly wasn't on the slope above the shed, so she must have made it over the brow of the hill to the north. He glanced at the sun.

It wasn't quite noon, he thought, but it was close. He started to run down the slope toward Amity, sick with the paralyzing fear that he would not be in time.

He heard the band playing "Turkey in the Straw" before he reached the first house. He was out of breath; he staggered and fell, and for a short time lay motionlessly on the ground, laboring for air, then he got back on his feet and ran more slowly toward his house.

He didn't know where to look for Jerry and he didn't have time to run all over town. He still didn't know who was to be murdered; he didn't know what he could do to get Jean out of the house, but maybe he could do something. Then a thought sent a chill down his back. Maybe he was too late. Maybe it was all over by now.

He reached the barn behind his house and slipped inside quickly. If any of the outlaws had been looking out of the kitchen window, they would have seen him, but it was a chance he had to take if he was going to get into the barn, and it was the only place where he could hide and still watch the house.

Bud pulled the door shut. The three horses were in the first three stalls, so it wasn't over with, but he couldn't guess how much time was left. Now he was here, he didn't know what to do. He had no weapon. What could an unarmed fourteen-year-old boy do against three killers?

He had been stupid even to dream that he might think of something. He had to go after Jerry whether he had time or not, had to find him and bring him here. He would think of something. Jerry would get Jean out of the house.

He started back toward the door, then stopped to glance through the cobweb-covered window. He froze. He was too late. They must have seen him.

Sammy had stepped through the back door and was crossing the yard toward the barn.

XXII

Corrigan took the Burlington road out of town, pushing his horse as hard as he could. He knew it would be touch and go, that it was almost twelve now and the tension would be tightening the nerves of the three outlaws in the Dugan house.

He wasn't sure he could make it back in time to be in the barn when Matt came into the house with the money. Alone, Matt would have no chance at all if he tried to smoke it out with the outlaws, but the fat would be in the fire and they'd be sure to take Jean with them.

Then he saw Dick Miles's rig top the ridge ahead of him and he breathed a little easier. Maybe luck was running his way now. He kept on up the road, holding his right hand over his head for the rig to stop. It kept coming and he motioned wildly. For a minute he thought Miles was going to run him down, but he finally stopped, yanking the horses back on their haunches and slamming on his brake.

"Get out of the way, Corrigan!" Miles bawled furiously. "I figured I was gonna make it to town by the skin of my teeth, and here you are holding me up."

A man with a white beard sat in the back seat beside a smooth-shaven young man. Both had rifles, and both seemed a little uncertain about whether they should start shooting or not. The bearded man would be Governor Ben Wyatt, but Corrigan had no idea who the other one was.

"Who is he?" Wyatt asked.

"The sheriff," Miles answered. "Jerry Corrigan."

"Well, young man," Wyatt said, "we were stopped once before this morning by three men who intended to shoot me. Why are you stopping us?"

"I'm trying to keep you from getting shot," Corrigan said quickly. "I haven't got much time to explain it to you, but Matt Dugan's family's safety is involved. Matt's, too, if I don't get back in a hurry. Just a few minutes ago we learned of a conspiracy to murder you when you get on the platform and start speaking."

Miles's expression showed he didn't believe it. He snorted: "Come off it, Corrigan. Matt's family would be. . . ."

"I told you we should never have come here!" the young man beside Wyatt shouted. "We should have got on the train in Burlington and gone back to Denver."

"I figure this one is a lot of hogwash, Governor," Miles said, "though I can't see what Corrigan's up to."

"Shut up, Miles," Corrigan said angrily. "I don't know why you're talking that way. All I want to do is to save the governor's life. I'm asking you to stay here for at least half an hour. Matt and me think that'll give us time to clean the outlaws. . . ."

"Hold on, Sheriff," Wyatt interrupted. "I've got something to say. Tom, we're not going back. I keep telling you that, and you keep talking about going back. Now then, Miles, do you know the sheriff pretty well?"

274

"Yeah, I know him, all right," Miles said grudgingly. "He's a purty fair lawman for a young buck, but there's some cowmen around Amity who don't want this dam project to be finished up. This might be their scheme to keep. . . ."

"My God, Miles," Corrigan said, "I knew you weren't smart, but I didn't think you were an idiot. I'm not going to stay here arguing. I've got to get back to town because Matt's heading for his house in a few minutes and he'll get shot all to hell if I ain't there to give him a hand."

"How did you hear about this conspiracy?" Wyatt asked, still unconvinced.

"An old man named Pete Fisher was in on it," Corrigan said. "I mean, it was Denver men who put it together, but Fisher was the one who told 'em about you coming and how easy it would be to shoot you from the front upstairs window of the Dugan house. He got religion this morning. Claimed he was sorry he ever got into it, so he told Matt all about it and wants it stopped. He'd been drinking enough for his tongue to be oiled up good. Matt had put up three strangers in his house since midnight, but they told him it was a scheme to rob the bank."

Wyatt nodded, obviously believing Corrigan's story now. "It makes sense. We received a warning to stay out of Amity. It's my guess Fisher sent it. When the time grew near for me to arrive, he got cold feet. I know Fisher and I know what he thinks of me, but I can understand why he wanted it stopped. He's not a killer. I think I know the Denver men you mention. They are killers. I suspect we'll find their names in Fisher's house and we'll have them arrested."

"Then you'll stay here for half an hour?" Corrigan demanded.

"We will stay a few minutes," Wyatt said stubbornly. "Not half an hour. I don't have that much time, and I don't want to disappoint the Amity people by keeping them waiting. If you haven't arrested these men by the time we reach town, I won't get up on the platform. I'll just. . . ."

"All right," Corrigan said, and whirled his horse and dug in the steel.

Time, he thought. Somehow Miles and the governor just couldn't understand how much each second counted. He should have ridden off and let them do what they pleased as soon as he had warned them, but, no, he'd waited until he had Wyatt's assurance they'd stay there for a while.

Matt would say he'd done right, that Wyatt

had to be persuaded to stay because his life was the important one, but Corrigan would never agree to that. If any life was more important than the others', it was Jean's.

Well, it was too late now to change what he'd done. As he rocketed down the slope and into the alley that ran behind the Dugan house, he glanced at the sun. If it wasn't high noon, it was within minutes of it. He didn't know just when Matt would take the money to the house, and, of course, there was no way of knowing how long the men would wait for the governor to show up.

Corrigan pulled his horse to a stop and dismounted. He turned the animal into a corral belonging to one of Matt's neighbors. He didn't want to stir up any dust or ride his horse back of the Dugan house. One of the men might be watching the alley from the kitchen window. It wouldn't take much to trigger an explosion if the outlaws were as jumpy by this time as he expected them to be.

He ran along the alley, then slowed up, reminding himself again that he didn't want to stir up any dust. He mentally cursed Dick Miles for not believing him. He had never liked Miles and was well aware that Miles didn't like him, mostly because Miles had courted Jean and lost.

Miles was a fool for thinking Jean would love a man twice her age, but being a fool was beside the point right now. Miles had not believed him, and that had made the governor doubtful, so several minutes had been wasted. Even worse was the possibility that, after they thought it over, they might decide it was just scare talk and come on into town.

Reaching the back of the barn, Corrigan slipped quickly around the corner, his revolver in his hand. Hugging the wall, he eased along it to the door, opened it, and stepped inside. He was following Matt's orders. He hadn't liked the idea in the first place and he still didn't like it. What was he supposed to do while he was here?

"Jerry, I sure am glad to see you."

Corrigan wheeled toward the far end of the runway. Bud Dugan was coming toward him, white-faced and trembling. He was covered with litter from the straw-covered floor of a stall. Corrigan, staring at him, was stunned by his appearance here in the Dugan barn.

"How'd you happen to be here?" Corrigan demanded. "I thought they had. . . ."

"The woman who was riding herd on me got scared and left after tying me up in

Uncle Pete Fisher's soddy," Bud said. "I got loose and ran here as fast as I could, but I didn't know what to do after I got here. I was going to hunt for you 'cause I knew you'd figure out what to do, but that Sammy came out and saddled their horses." Bud swallowed. "I didn't have a gun. Jerry, I never was so scared in my life. I figured he seen me come in and was gonna kill me. He hadn't seen me, though. I hid in the last stall and he never went back that far, so he didn't find me."

"I'm glad you're safe," Corrigan said. "Your dad's been worried about you."

He turned to the window and stared at the back of the house. He didn't see anyone. Nothing moved, but Jean was inside. She had to be. They wouldn't turn her loose. He could only hope she was still alive and unharmed. Now that it was too late, he could blame himself for not doing something about it this morning when he'd been in the house with her.

Bud gripped his arm. "What are you gonna do, Jerry? I wanted to get loose so I could come and tell you what was going on, but I guess you know."

"I know, all right," Corrigan said dully, "but that don't tell me what to do."

Here he was, fifty feet from the back door

of the house, and he couldn't risk showing himself until he knew where Jean was. He had to do something. For a few seconds he was sick with the agony of indecision. If he could slip through a neighbor's yard until he was opposite the porch and then run to the back door . . . if he could just get inside so he could see Jean and know that she was all right, he. . . .

He heard a rifle shot, the sharp, brittle *crack* coming from inside the house as he could judge. He had no idea what it meant unless Miles had come on into town with the governor and the outlaws had seen him and shot him.

But it couldn't be that way, he told himself. It couldn't be. That was what Matt was trying to prevent.

XXIII

John Smith looked at his watch. One minute until twelve o'clock. He noticed that his hand trembled slightly as he shoved the watch back into his pocket. He had never really been nervous in his life before as a critical moment approached, but he was nervous now. He felt hollow all the way down deep into his belly.

So much depended on these next few

minutes, and yet it was a situation that could not be pinned down to an exact minute. There were too many variables. The big one, of course, was the time it would take the governor to drive from Burlington to Amity.

Another point that bothered him a little was the time Dugan would arrive at the house with the money from the bank. He didn't care if Dugan was late, or even if he didn't come at all. The instant the governor was shot, the three of them would pull out in a hurry, but if Dugan got here before Ross Hart fired the fatal shot, someone would have to watch him as well as Jean. The simplest way to handle it would be to tie him up. It would take a few minutes for him to free himself and a few minutes was all they'd need.

Jean was baking something in the kitchen. She was humming, apparently unconcerned about what was happening and might even happen to her. She glanced at him and smiled and kept on with what she was doing. She was a cool one, he thought, a lot cooler than her mother was.

The morning had passed without any trouble once the young squirt of a sheriff was out of the house. Smith had been afraid he'd come back. He was the kind of man

Smith feared because he was young and in love with the girl and likely to be jumpy. But he hadn't returned. Jean hadn't give them any trouble at all, and now the moment they'd been waiting for was here, or would be here any second and they'd be on their way.

Smith turned and walked back into the front room. Sammy Bean was slouched on the couch, his legs stretched in front of him. He had just come back from saddling the horses. All clear in the barn, he'd said. Nobody in the alley. There wouldn't be, of course. Anyone who could walk was in front of the courthouse by this time, waiting to see the governor.

"We could take the girl," Smith said. "That would be one way to keep the sheriff and Dugan from giving us a run."

"No," Sammy said. "She'd slow us up. They won't give us a run on account of the boy. If they do, we'll take him along."

Smith nodded, knowing that Sammy was right. He wasn't sure why he had even suggested it because he had thought of it before and discarded the idea for the very reason Sammy had mentioned. He guessed that he was more nervous than he had realized. The number one objective was to get out of Amity in a hurry once the governor was taken care of and he'd better remember it.

"Keep an eye on the girl," Smith said. "I'm going up to see Ross."

He turned toward the stairs and climbed to the hall on the second floor. He decided that it wasn't nervousness that had made him suggest taking Jean when they left. The real reason was he didn't fully trust Dolly. If the boy got away from her, or if she panicked and left him in the soddy, he'd get clear and they wouldn't have a hostage.

Even if that happened, Jean would still slow them up and the loss of even two or three minutes at that point might be fatal. No, they'd play it out just the way it had been planned. They had spent hours going over every move they would make. Now he was surprised at himself, the cold, calculating John Smith, for even suggesting the change in plan to Sammy Bean.

Ross Hart sat close to the open window, his Winchester in his hands, his gaze on the crowd that was milling around in front of the platform. The band was playing a toe-tapping tune of some kind. Smith thought it was "Arkansas Traveler," although he wasn't sure. He'd never had much music sense and often had trouble naming a tune that was familiar.

Hart glanced at him and quickly turned

his gaze back to the crowd. He said: "The old booger's late."

"It's a long ways to Burlington," Smith said. "They couldn't call it right to the minute."

"No, guess not," Hart said. "Well, one thing is sure. Old man Fisher picked the right house for us. I couldn't miss at this distance."

He was a cold one, this Ross Hart. He looked as if he were actually going to enjoy killing a man. Smith took his handkerchief out of his pocket and wiped his face. Hart didn't notice. If he had, Smith would have passed it off with a remark about the day being hot. But it wasn't the heat. Damn it, the thing was he wanted it over with and he wanted to get out of this stinking, one-horse town. For that matter, he wanted to get clear out of Colorado.

He thought of all the years he had lived in Denver and walked the narrow line between the underworld and the world of legitimate business, with one foot in each. He had let himself be used by stronger, tougher men than he was, and they were the ones who had made the profit. He was always the front man, the smooth-tongued one, the go-between.

Smith reminded himself that he had never

in his whole life made a really big deal, enough to get out of the country and stay out, enough to go to South America and live like a king. This time he had the big deal; he had bargained to kill a man. That was the reason he was able to force the size of pay-off that he had.

It had been dangerous, damned dangerous right from the moment they had walked into the back of the Dugan house and made a prisoner of Nora Dugan. Because all of them knew it would be dangerous, he had been able to drive a hard bargain, and now he would have the money to go anywhere he wanted to.

He wiped his face again, his thoughts coming back to the job that had not yet been done. Wyatt was indeed late. Too late, and now a new worry began working into Smith's consciousness. Suppose someone had caught on and was keeping the governor out of town? No, it didn't add up. Dugan or Corrigan might figure out what was happening, or make a wild guess, but both would play it out as ordered because neither wanted Jean to be harmed.

"You haven't seen a rig come into town?" Smith asked.

"No."

Hart said the word sharply as if the waiting was finally getting to him. Then, seconds later, he leaned forward in his chair. He whispered: "There he is."

Hart brought the Winchester to his shoulder, held it there a moment, and squeezed off a shot. "Got him," he said with satisfaction, and was up and out of his chair and halfway across the room to the door before Smith could move.

They ran along the hall and down the stairs, boot heels cracking sharply on the floor. Sammy Bean was already in the kitchen, calling back: "I'll get the horses!"

For the moment Smith had completely forgotten about the money Matt Dugan was to bring to the house, but now, as he rushed across the front room, he saw Dugan standing in the hall doorway, staring at him as if he were completely bewildered. A satchel was in his hand. Smith whirled to him and yanked the satchel away from him.

"Don't come after us," Smith warned. "Don't forget we've got the kid. If I see any dust behind us, I'll put a bullet through his head."

He wheeled away and raced into the kitchen. He plunged headlong across it and on to the back porch, suddenly realizing that Jean should have been standing there beside the range, but she wasn't in sight.

XXIV

Matt Dugan had hesitated about taking the money to the house for the simple reason that it was something he didn't want to do, so he put it off. Once the outlaws had it, the chance of getting it back was pretty slim. The dam project would be finished. Done for. He had known it all the time, of course, but it hit him harder than ever now that the moment was here. It was like burying a cherished dream.

He couldn't do it. Pete Fisher had told him it was just an excuse, that the three outlaws had come to Amity to kill the governor, not to rob the bank. So the seconds dragged out, with Matt looking at his watch every minute until it was fifteen after twelve.

He could not delay any longer. Maybe the $10,000 was only the frosting on the cake, but Jean and Bud were prisoners, he had been ordered to bring the money, and suddenly he felt guilty for not doing it.

Matt opened a desk drawer, took out the .45 he kept there, checked it quickly and saw that there were five shells in the cylinder, then slipped it under his waistband on his left side, with the butt to the front. He buttoned his coat and, carrying the satchel that contained the money in his left hand, hurried out of the bank.

The customers had finally cleared out. Fred Follett had locked the front door and was working in the teller's cage. He glanced curiously at Matt as he strode past, but asked no questions. Matt unlocked the front door, called to Follett — "Lock it after me!" — and stepped outside.

He wasn't sure that Follett knew what was in the satchel, but it didn't make any difference. It would all come out soon enough. He hurried along Main Street toward his house, half running now that he was late because he had lingered so long in his office and he was afraid they would harm Jean because of his tardiness. But there was one good thing about his having wasted those fifteen minutes. Jerry Corrigan had been given time to stop Dick Miles and get back to town and be in the barn.

Matt still didn't know how it would work. Jerry might have been right in saying Matt would get himself killed, but at this particular moment Matt didn't much care if he could take the outlaws with him. That was going to take some doing.

He slipped his right hand under his coat, wrapped his fingers around the butt of the revolver, and pulled it out from under the waistband, then slipped it back. He had never been one to practice his draw, so he wasn't a gunman, proud of his speed. Still, he was a good shot, and, if it worked out so Jerry could get into the fight, there was an excellent chance they could take the three men.

Matt hoped he could see Jean and know she was all right before he opened up. He was a little sick when his thoughts jumped from Jean to Bud because he had no way of knowing what would happen to the boy if the outlaws failed to show up on schedule.

Bud's life might be sacrificed just as Matt's might and possibly even Jean's, and then for some reason that eluded him he thought of the Bible story about Abraham who had been told to sacrifice his son Isaac. He began to run, anger boiling up in him until he was filled with an unreasoning rage.

He raced up the path to his front door, yanked the screen open, and plunged into the hall. That was when he heard the *crack* of the rifle from upstairs. He stopped, stunned, as he heard boots pound along the hall above him and down the stairs; he saw Sammy Bean jump up from the couch and run out of the house through the kitchen.

All that Matt could think of was that Governor Wyatt had not stayed out of town in spite of Jerry Corrigan's warning, and, because he had been too stubborn to take the warning, he had been killed. Ross Hart rushed past him toward the back door, Smith jerked the satchel out of his hand and warned him not to follow them, and ran after Hart.

Matt came out of it then, thinking he had not seen Jean. She might be alive, or they might have killed or raped her, but they weren't taking her with them. He drew his gun as he ran through the kitchen. When he reached the back door, he glimpsed Corrigan step out of the barn, with Sammy Bean only a few feet from him; he saw the burst of powder flame from the muzzle of Corrigan's gun and he saw Bean go down.

In that moment Matt Dugan felt a burst of exultation. They had the outlaws; they had them in a crossfire from which there was no escape. Ross Hart and John Smith were caught between the house and the barn, but they were closer to the house and both wheeled to rush back into the house.

Even as Hart made the turn, he must have realized he was being stupid. He couldn't outrun Corrigan's bullet, so he whirled back and fired with his rifle that he held at his hip. Corrigan took a shot at him. Both missed, and then Matt, standing in the back door, pulled the trigger of his .45. He shot Hart in the back as coldly and with as little remorse as he would have gunned down a mad dog.

Now John Smith, his face twisted by the terrifying knowledge that he was a dead man, must have realized he was caught here in the open between two men who had nothing but contempt and hate for him. He tried desperately to bring his gun into play, but time had run out for him.

Matt and Jerry fired in the same second. Smith's gun, half lifted, drove a slug into one of the steps below the back door. With one bullet in his chest and another smashing through his spine from the back, he was dead before he hit the ground, his lifeless body falling across the satchel of money that he had dropped when he had clawed wildly for his gun.

For just a moment Matt stood there, with powder smoke forming a cloud in the back yard, then it drifted slowly away as the final echoes of the gunshots died. He saw Bud come out of the barn and for an instant he felt the weakness of relief that swept over him, then the thought came to him that this must be a crazy nightmare that suddenly was turning out all right. Jean was beside him a moment later, an arm going around him.

"I'm fine," she said. "I hid in the pantry and locked the door when I heard the shot. I didn't know what was happening, but I was afraid they'd take me with them when they left and I had an idea they'd pull out right after that first shot. When I heard them run out of the house, I knew I was right."

Bud came walking across the yard toward Matt who stepped to the ground and laid a hand on the boy's shoulder. He said hoarsely: "Thank God you're alive." Tears rolled down his cheeks as he shoved his gun under his waistband and put his other arm around Jean. Jerry Corrigan was there then, and Matt let him have Jean.

He tried to smile at Bud, but the smile wouldn't come. All he could say was: "It must have been bad, wasn't it, boy?"

And Bud said: "It wasn't any fun and that's a fact."

Matt picked up the satchel and they went inside. Corrigan asked: "Who do you suppose they shot? I stopped Miles and told them what was going on. Wyatt promised to wait a while. He wouldn't say how long."

"We'd better see," Matt said.

"I'll stay here," Jean said, white-faced. "I got through the morning, but I'm at the end of the line. I think I'll have a good cry. Just go away and leave me."

Matt tossed the satchel on the couch and went outside, jerking his head at Corrigan and Bud to follow him. They met Nora who was running to the house from the Methodist church. Matt said: "They're all right, both of them." She stopped to hug Bud, then hurried on into the house.

"She'll have a good cry, too," Matt said. "It'll make both of them feel better."

Corrigan said — "Yeah." — as if he might indulge in the same. Suddenly Matt felt like laughing and wondered if he was hysterical. He looked at Bud and shook his head. The boy had come through it the best of any of them.

When they reached the crowd, Corrigan took the lead, shouldering through the mass of people with Matt and Bud close behind. Corrigan kept saying: "It's the sheriff. Let me through. It's the sheriff."

When they reached the platform, they found Cole Talbot and Jim Long and several others standing beside a body that was covered by a canvas. A hush had fallen over the crowd and no one understood what had happened or seemed to know what to do. It was just as well that people didn't know the whole story, Matt thought.

The dead man was Uncle Pete Fisher. When Matt lifted the canvas to look at the body, he saw that Fisher had been hit dead center in the chest. Blood had spread across his shirt from the bullet hole.

"Did he say anything after he was shot?" Matt asked.

Talbot shook his head. "Not a word. He had just jumped up on the platform and held up his hands as if he wanted to say something, but he didn't have a chance. We moved him off the platform to the ground. Doc was right here, but there wasn't anything he could do."

"Cole, you and Jerry move the body to the coroner's office," Matt said. "The governor's going to be here any minute. Jim, you introduce him when he gets here and tell the people that Jerry nailed the men who killed Uncle Pete."

"What about those other shots that came later?" Talbot asked.

"That was when we nailed the men who got Uncle Pete," Corrigan said. "All right, Cole. Let's get this body out of here before the governor sees it."

Matt's eyes locked with Corrigan's. They were thinking the same thing, he told himself, that Pete Fisher, remorseful over his part in the murder plot, had jumped up on the platform, knowing that the killer who was waiting for Ben Wyatt to appear would see his white beard and mistake him for Wyatt.

"I've got to make an explanation to these people," Long said worriedly.

Some of it has to be told, Matt thought. He nodded, and said: "There was a plot to murder the governor and the killer made the mistake of taking Uncle Pete for the governor."

Matt turned away as Dick Miles's rig appeared around the corner. The band had started to play again, ragged music but better than no music at all. Matt asked several men to move the bodies of the dead outlaws to the coroner's office. He made no explanation to the men who went to the house with him beyond saying that the dead outlaws were the ones who had shot Uncle Pete Fisher.

As soon as the men left with the bodies, Matt stepped into the house and picked up the satchel. He found Nora and Jean sitting on the couch, white-faced and dry-eyed.

The tears will come later, he thought. He lingered only long enough to say: "Pete Fisher is the man they shot. They must have mistaken him for the governor."

He went out through the front door and walked rapidly toward the bank, wanting to lock up the money in the safe as soon as he could. The whole story would come out in time, but right now he didn't feel like making an explanation to anyone. He wasn't sure he had done right. All he knew was that everything had turned out better than he had hoped an hour ago.

Now, walking along the side of the courthouse square, he heard the governor's booming voice: "You people are to be congratulated for this fine accomplishment. Republicans, Democrats, and Populists would agree on one thing. As long as men and women in our great state of Colorado have the initiative that it takes to raise enough money to carry through a fine project like this. . . ."

Matt hurried on to the bank. He would lock the money in the safe and get back to the courthouse in time to hear the end of the speech. He would shake the governor's hand and thank him for coming to Amity; they would have lunch and the band would play some more and later there would be dancing in the Masonic Temple.

Then Matt took a long breath. He thought: *My children have not been hurt. The governor is alive. We still have the money to finish the dam.*

He could ask for nothing more.

ABOUT THE AUTHOR

Wayne D. Overholser won three Spur Awards from the Western Writers of America and has a long list of fine Western titles to his credit. He was born in Pomeroy, Washington, and attended the University of Montana, University of Oregon, and the University of Southern California before becoming a public schoolteacher and principal in various Oregon communities. He began writing for Western pulp magazines in 1936 and within a couple of years was a regular contributor to Street & Smith's *Western Story Magazine* and Fiction House's *Lariat Story Magazine. Buckaroo's Code* (1947) was his first Western novel and remains one of his best. In the 1950s and 1960s, having retired from academic work to concentrate on writing, he would publish as many as four books a year under his own name or a pseudonym, most prominently as Joseph Wayne. *The Violent Land* (1954), *The*

Lone Deputy (1957), *The Bitter Night* (1961), and *Riders of the Sundowns* (1997) are among the finest of the Overholser titles. *The Sweet and Bitter Land* (1950), *Bunch Grass* (1955), and *Land of Promises* (1962) are among the best Joseph Wayne titles, and *Law Man* (1953) is a most rewarding novel under the Lee Leighton pseudonym. Overholser's Western novels, whatever the byline, are based on a solid knowledge of the history and customs of the 19th-Century West, particularly when set in his two favorite Western states, Oregon and Colorado. Many of his novels are first-person narratives, a technique that tends to bring an added dimension of vividness to the frontier experiences of his narrators and frequently, as in *Cast a Long Shadow* (1957), the female characters one encounters are among the most memorable. He wrote his numerous novels with a consistent skill and an uncommon sensitivity to the depths of human character. Almost invariably, his stories weave a spell of their own with their scenes and images of social and economic forces often in conflict and the diverse ways of life and personalities that made the American Western frontier so unique a time and place in human history. *The Durango Stage* will be his next Five Star Western.